"Now it's my turn to be entertained. Play your fiddle for me, Sarah," Jamie commanded.

She bowed in mock obedience. "Why does the word *laird* come to mind?" she asked, then began to concentrate on playing the tune. But right in the middle she noticed that the bed was shaking and Jamie had his arm over his face.

"You beast," she said in hot indignation. "You had me play so you could laugh at me!"

He shook his head vigorously in denial, but muffled, choking sounds that resembled laughter escaped his mouth.

Sarah put down the fiddle and leaped on him, pummeling and shaking him. "Rude, horrible, tactless man . . ."

He grabbed her hands to protect himself. "Stop, stop," he begged. Then he rolled so that Sarah was beneath him on the bed and he lay across her.

Sarah went very still and her eyes grew large. She'd felt so close to Jamie, it had seemed perfectly natural to wrestle playfully with him. But now, lying under him, she knew the time for play had passed. She was aching for him, and he for her, and the risk didn't seem to matter any longer. . . .

WHAT ARE *LOVESWEPT* ROMANCES?

They are stories of true romance and touching emotion. We believe those two very important ingredients are constants in our highly sensual and very believable stories in the *LOVESWEPT* line. Our goal is to give you, the reader, stories of consistently high quality that may sometimes make you laugh, sometimes make you cry, but are always fresh and creative and contain many delightful surprises within their pages.

Most romance fans read an enormous number of books. Those they truly love, they keep. Others may be traded with friends and soon forgotten. We hope that each *LOVESWEPT* romance will be a treasure—a "keeper." We will always try to publish

LOVE STORIES YOU'LL NEVER FORGET
BY AUTHORS YOU'LL ALWAYS REMEMBER

The Editors

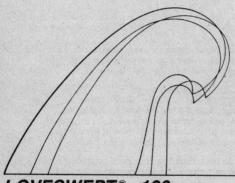

LOVESWEPT® • 186
Susan Richardson
Fiddlin' Fool

BANTAM BOOKS
TORONTO • NEW YORK • LONDON • SYDNEY • AUCKLAND

FIDDLIN' FOOL

A Bantam Book / April 1987

LOVESWEPT® and the wave device are registered trademarks of Bantam Books, Inc. Registered in U.S. Patent and Trademark Office and elsewhere.

All rights reserved.
Copyright © 1987 by Susan Richardson.
Cover art copyright © 1987 by Bantam Books, Inc.
This book may not be reproduced in whole or in part, by mimeograph or any other means, without permission.
For information address: Bantam Books, Inc.

If you would be interested in receiving protective vinyl covers for your Loveswept books, please write to this address for information:

Loveswept
Bantam Books
P.O. Box 985
Hicksville, NY 11802

ISBN 0-553-21810-7

Published simultaneously in the United States and Canada

Bantam Books are published by Bantam Books, Inc. Its trademark, consisting of the words "Bantam Books" and the portrayal of a rooster, is registered in U.S. Patent and Trademark Office and in other countries. Marca Registrada. Bantam Books, Inc., 666 Fifth Avenue, New York, New York 10103.

PRINTED IN THE UNITED STATES OF AMERICA

O   0 9 8 7 6 5 4 3 2 1

One

"Sarah! Over here!"

Sarah's head swiveled as she searched for the source of the sound in the press of people maneuvering toward their seats in the crowded auditorium. She knew by the voice it was Pam, but she couldn't find her.

"There," said Michael, one of the housemates Sarah had dragged along to this concert of Celtic fiddling. "In green. And isn't that the man himself with her?"

Sarah's gaze searched the area Michael was pointing at and came to rest, not on her red-haired friend Pam, one of the organizers of the concert, but on the astonishing man beside her. It was indeed the man they'd come to hear—the famous Jamie McLeod, Scottish fiddler extraordinaire.

Sarah had stared at his face on album covers so often he should have looked familiar. And the face was the same, with its strong chin and the lines connecting his slash of a nose to a wide, expressive mouth. But he was huge—at least six feet five and

1

2 • SUSAN RICHARDSON

two-hundred-plus hard-packed pounds. She hadn't expected that. And his hair was different—longer and paler than in the photographs. He was a true towhead. The incongruity of his powerful frame and that shaggy head of little-boy hair made her grin.

"Michael, why don't you and Tom find our seats?" she suggested, without taking her eyes off Jamie McLeod. "I'll just say hello to Pam."

Michael grunted, managing through long practice to make even that sound sardonic. He'd seen Sarah's eyes widen at the sight of the big fiddler, and he didn't think it was Pam she was interested in.

Sarah was still smiling as she approached Pam and her star performer.

Jamie McLeod was watching Sarah with interest, noting swiftly that she was small, blond, and adorable. He noted, too, that something about him was amusing her. He grinned back and nodded his head, eyebrows raised as if to say, "We'll discuss this later, if you please."

Pam reached for Sarah's hand and drew her to her side in her usual warm way. "Sarah," she said, "I knew you'd want to meet Jamie. I've just been telling him you're one of his biggest fans."

Sarah winced humorously at the description. She loved his music, true, but *fan* implied a whole host of qualities she wasn't sure she wanted to lay claim to. At her expression, Jamie McLeod's grin widened wickedly.

"A fan, are you?" he teased in his deep, lilting voice as he reached for her hand. "Does that mean you've come for my autograph?" His accent was like music.

FIDDLIN' FOOL • 3

"Is it worth money?" Sarah quipped, tilting her head to one side.

By then his large, warm hand had closed around her small one. It was a good thing she'd already gotten her answer out, she thought, because with the touch of his fingers, she became mute. She stared up at him and felt the breath driven from her lungs. She could think of nothing but the feel of his skin and the warmth emanating from his body. Heat flooded through her veins. She was suddenly and shockingly too aware of his body—and of her own—to play her assigned part in this scene.

If Jamie had made another remark requiring an answer, she'd have been in trouble. But he didn't. He looked down into her wide, startled eyes, and his smile faded as his gaze grew intent. Here now, he thought. What was this?

Beside them, and in another world, Pam said confidentially, "She is a fan, really, Jamie. She won't admit it because she thinks it's undignified."

His hand convulsively squeezed Sarah's, then he let go and turned his attention to Pam.

"No, Pam," he said, feigning sadness, "a real fan would be gushing and telling me she had all my albums. You've still not found me a real fan."

Sarah was grateful for the teasing exchange between the other two. It gave her time to pull herself together. When Jamie's hand had dropped hers, her perspective had shifted back to normal, just as suddenly as it had spun the other way at his touch.

What was *that*? she asked herself in disbelief. The effect was something like an earthquake, when one's steady foundations became fluid and unstable, then, abruptly, it was over and one wondered what had hap-

4 · SUSAN RICHARDSON

pened. Jamie's touch caused a reaction in her of about 7.3 on the Richter scale, and she had better get out of here fast in case of aftershocks.

"Actually, Jamie," Pam was saying treacherously, "Sarah has two copies of some of your albums. She was afraid she'd wear one out and not be able to replace it."

Sarah was feeling more normal, but she was afraid her voice wouldn't be quite steady yet, so she just nodded and shrugged, admitting it.

With a smile for Sarah, Jamie said, "Well, then, that's two real live fans I have." Dryly he added, "The other's my granny."

Sarah laughed, a low gurgling sound. How nice that he could make fun of himself.

Jamie's smile deepened. He liked her voice. It had a husky quality that gave it a warmth to match her smile. Her skin was warm, too, with a peachy tone to it. Only her silvery-gray eyes were cool. Contradictory messages.

He was completely engrossed in his inventory, and Sarah found herself ensnared by clear blue eyes that missed nothing. She felt heat creeping over her once more, and with it came a panic. It was the aftershock! she told herself in alarm.

Again Pam saved her. "I'm a fan, too, Jamie, so that makes three. And after the concert there should be two or three hundred more."

Sarah seized the opportunity to excuse herself. "I'm sure you have things to do to get ready," she said quickly to Jamie. "It was good to meet you. I'd better find my friends now." She was backing away as she spoke, to avoid shaking hands again, and Jamie was watching her quizzically. She had the

FIDDLIN' FOOL • 5

feeling he knew exactly what effect he had on her. "See you later, Pam," she added.

Jamie gave her a meaningful look and said as if she'd spoken to him, "Yes, see you later. Run along now." He put a slight emphasis on the word "run" and grinned at the indignant look she threw him over her shoulder.

Sarah saw Michael and Tom sitting in the fourth row and scolded herself all the way to her seat. You're being absurd! she told herself. You're twenty-six, not sixteen! Too old for crushes. But she knew it wasn't that. She didn't feel like a young girl staring at her idol on high. She felt as if she and Jamie McLeod were already friends. Well . . . maybe not exactly friends. But as if they had a bond, were important to each other in some way.

She shook her head in self-disgust. Don't dramatize, Sarah, she lectured silently. He's just a devastatingly attractive man, that's all. With more charm than you can handle. Forget it. Enjoy the music. It's the music you came for, remember?

Tom smiled and stood to let Sarah reach the seat between him and Michael. "Can you see okay?"

"Fine, fine," she answered so testily that Tom adjusted his glasses and looked at her in bewildered surprise, wondering what he'd done.

Half an hour later, tears ran unnoticed down Sarah's face as the music, an ancient Scottish lament, swirled around her.

Seated alone in a wedge of light on the stage was tall towheaded Jamie with his fiddle tucked beneath his chin. His eyes were closed and on his face was a look of deep concentration.

6 · SUSAN RICHARDSON

The bow drew a last lonely wail from the fiddle and was still. As the sound died away, Sarah released a breath she hadn't realized she was holding. What pain there was in this music! she thought. And what beauty. Something wild and free in it tugged at her like no other music she'd ever heard. And no one had ever played music like Jamie McLeod. He was a magician with the fiddle, making even the most rapid-fire series of notes sound clear and true.

Jamie didn't wait for applause. His light blue eyes surveyed what he could see of the audience with good-humored amusement. "And now while you all mop up," he said cheerfully, "I'll lighten the atmosphere here in Palo Alto."

His foot tapped as his bow moved in the quick jogging rhythm of a reel.

Sarah stiffened at his words. The nerve of him—to move them all to tears and then mock them for it!

She stared at the stage, her chin tilted belligerently, and intercepted a teasing grin. It wasn't the first time their eyes had met during the concert.

She returned a look of humorous affront, and Jamie's grin widened. She made him feel like smiling, he mused. His eyes kept seeking out her gamin face and fluffy golden hair in the audience. Angel hair. A small, sexy angel. He was playing to her, and he knew it. He also knew he'd never played better.

Now he watched her expression change from wounded pride to sheer happy response to the music. Oh, my, he said to himself. Oh my, oh my.

He wouldn't at all mind staying with her tonight, he thought as his fingers dealt automatically with the strings and bow. He could cancel the room reserved for him.

FIDDLIN' FOOL · 7

That brought him up short. You must be daft! he told himself. You've just met the girl. And what about the two guardians flanking her?

He sized them up as he played—a short dark fellow and a brown-haired one wearing glasses. The dark one was whispering in her ear just now. Well, it doesn't matter, he thought. They haven't a chance.

His gaze remained on Sarah throughout the reel. She sat still, small and erect, a puzzled expression on her face. Ah, he thought, she feels it too.

"That was a Kilbrech reel," he said into the microphone when he was finished and the applause died down. "It originated in my home village some years ago. A musicologist fellow came around wanting to tape the old songs of the region. We had none of our own, but we hated to disappoint the man, so my cousins and I made up that one."

A ripple of laughter met this Caledonian tall tale. He grinned, seeing the quick smile light Sarah's face. He wanted to keep telling jokes, just to see her smile.

"It's in all the recent collections of old reels now," he added shamelessly.

One hand adjusted the tuning knobs of his fiddle while he plucked the strings with the other hand, his head tilted to listen. To cover the time it was taking him to tune the instrument, he said, "My fiddle talks to me. Right now it's saying it doesn't want to play a tune in the key of B flat." The audience laughed.

Jamie grinned companionably, still struggling with the knobs. "It's a young fiddle," he said. "Not trained yet. My old fiddle never talked back."

Sarah leaned toward Michael. "Isn't he charming?" she whispered.

8 · SUSAN RICHARDSON

Michael's voice ascended to a falsetto whisper. "Oh, yes, he's just precious!" he agreed facetiously.

Sarah grimaced with humor. "Idiot!" she said equably, and turned away. Michael grinned cheerfully.

As Jamie began another piece, Sarah studied him, trying to pinpoint what it was about him that had such a powerful effect on her.

His clothes were ordinary enough: corduroy pants and a blue shirt with the sleeves rolled up.

His face was anything but ordinary. Not a strictly handsome face, but a strong and arresting one.

Then there was the body, of course. His size alone would have made him remarkable. That and his sheer male presence. Every slow, easy movement spoke of control and virility. He exuded a kind of sexuality that few women would be unaware of, Sarah thought. Was that it? Simple sex appeal? Somehow she doubted it.

The concert finally came to an end. After two encores, Jamie rose and held up his hand in acknowledgment. "Thank you," he said. "Thank you all for coming. There's nothing more embarrassing than playing to empty chairs." He paused as the audience laughed.

He pointed with his bow to the back of the auditorium. "There are a few things on the back table for sale. Maps of Scotland. Tins of my granny's famous shortbread. And, oh, yes," he added as if he'd just remembered, "a few albums by assorted musicians, name of McLeod. Someone will be there to relieve you of your money. Good night to you all."

The house lights came up. People stood and gathered their coats as a buzz of conversation grew.

Jamie stepped off the small stage and was quickly

surrounded. Over the crowd of people around him, he mimed a message to Sarah. "Wait!"

She smiled beatifically as she rose. She had no intention of leaving.

At Sarah's side, Michael eyed her keenly, his expression uneasy. The look in her eyes wasn't typical of the cool, level-headed Sarah he knew.

"Well, what did you think?" Tom asked, stretching and smiling genially at Sarah and Michael.

"Where have you been?" Michael asked. "Sarah's bewitched. She's in a trance, practically swooning over our Scottish swain here, and you ask if she liked the concert."

"Shut up," Sarah said sweetly, not in the least perturbed. "Don't you recognize a music lover when you see one?"

Michael snorted. "I recognize a lover," he said, nodding significantly in Jamie's direction. "And I think he's spotted you as an easy victim."

Sarah ignored this. She had other things on her mind at the moment. Jamie was making a slow beeline toward her. He was talking to and smiling at assorted well-wishers, but he shed them inexorably as he threaded his way closer to her. She waited, a strange excitement growing in her.

Finally he was smiling down at her in silent satisfaction. She smiled back. It might have turned into another deep-gazing episode, but Michael, never known for tact, broke in.

"We know your name, would you like to know ours?" he asked, puffing out his chest and bristling slightly. Sarah hid a smile at Michael's brotherly belligerence.

Jamie evidently had no defensiveness in his make-

10 • SUSAN RICHARDSON

up. He smiled at Michael with easy good humor. "That would be very nice," he said, and turned back to Sarah. "I only know your first name."

"Sarah Hughes," she supplied.

"Ah, a good Celtic name," he said, his eyes twinkling.

"And Michael Ross." Michael stuck out his hand aggressively.

Jamie accepted it with a nod and the hint of an amused smile.

"This is Tom Hunter," Sarah said, propelling Tom forward. He held out a large, amiable paw and smiled his shy smile.

"Very nice music," he said.

"Thank you very much indeed," Jamie replied. Looking at Sarah, he added, "It was a good audience."

"It's the first time I've heard you play unaccompanied," she said. "All your records include other musicians. I think I prefer you solo."

His eyes lit with mischief. "Careful," he warned her. "You're sounding suspiciously like a fan."

Her laugh rippled out. "I think I've been thoroughly exposed by now."

"Can I buy you a drink or something?" he asked her. "I have to take good care of my fans, you know, having only the three."

Sarah glanced quickly at her housemates. They had come in her car and she couldn't just jettison them. She wasn't sure she was quite ready to go off with Jamie McLeod, either. She made a quick and typically careful decision. "Would you like to come back to our place for a drink and something to eat?" she asked.

Jamie nodded his pleased agreement. "I'd like that very much indeed. I'll just be gathering up my things. Will I meet you out front?"

FIDDLIN' FOOL • 11

As Sarah, Michael, and Tom walked out to the parking lot, Michael shook his head in disbelief. "For heaven's sake, Sarah," he said. "Do you know what you're doing? Stray cats are one thing, stray fiddlers another!" Sarah's propensity for rescuing strays was legendary.

She smiled, amused and not the least disturbed by this outburst. " 'Stray fiddler.' I like that."

"It's not a joke! You don't know anything about that man."

Her eyes flashed, but her voice remained reasonable. "I'm just inviting a new friend over for a drink, Michael. We've all done it dozens of times. If you don't like him, you don't have to help entertain him."

"That's not the point, and you know it!"

Her voice now ominously calm, Sarah asked, "What is the point, Michael?"

"The point is, that that fiddler isn't looking at you or thinking of you as a friend."

"All right." Her clipped tone and tight lips showed her anger. "Then I'm inviting a potential boyfriend over for a drink."

She stared defiantly at Michael, and even spared a glare for poor Tom, who was biting his lip and looking as if he'd like to say something but didn't dare.

Michael shook his head in defeat. "What can I say?" he muttered. "I know that obstinate look of yours."

When Jamie joined the three friends in the parking lot, one glance at Sarah's high color and Michael's sullen glower told him the guardians had been issuing warnings. His lips twitched, but he merely said cheerfully, "Here we are, then. All set?"

"All set," Sarah replied with determination.

12 · SUSAN RICHARDSON

Michael looked meaningfully from the duffel bag, tweed jacket, and fiddle case in Jamie's hands to Sarah. She lifted her chin stubbornly, but the sight of Jamie with all his belongings did alarm her a bit, if she were honest with herself.

Was he expecting to spend the night? Where was this lightning-fast attraction leading her? She'd allowed herself to be carried along on the tide of his fascination for her, which was unusual, to say the least.

The four of them piled into Sarah's vintage station wagon, Tom and Michael in back. With his fiddle case Jamie filled the front seat as thoroughly as if the big old car had been a new subcompact model. Sarah smiled at him, the pleasure she felt in his presence banishing doubts for the moment.

She glanced in the rearview mirror. "All aboard back there?" she asked, wanting to heal the breach with Michael. Receiving affirmative answers, she put the car into gear and pulled out of the parking lot.

Jamie lay a long arm across the back of the seat and twisted his body so that he was facing Sarah and could see into the back of the car as well.

"Are you all related, then?" he asked.

Sarah gave her characteristic gurgling chuckle. "Yes, don't you see the family resemblance?"

This was ridiculous. Tom was almost as big as Jamie; she and Michael were small, but absolute opposites in coloring and features. Michael had heavy features; her face was fine-boned and delicate, though the gray eyes were large and her mouth generous.

"We're housemates, and friends," she explained.

She sensed Jamie's smile of satisfaction as the lights of the university town south of San Francisco flashed by.

FIDDLIN' FOOL • 13

"It's Sarah's house," Michael said. "We're lowly tenants."

Tom's gentle bass chuckle rumbled through the car. "That's right. First and last month's rent and a cleaning deposit."

"Which you will never see again," Sarah said tartly. To Jamie, she added, "You've never met such pigs. If I'd had any idea, neither one of them would have gotten through the door."

Tom leaned toward Jamie. "Actually, we all lived in the house as tenants when we were graduate students, which Michael and I still are. And probably will be the rest of our lives," he added gloomily. "When Sarah turned twenty-one, she got access to a trust fund set up by her parents and bought the place."

Sarah's dimples flashed. "The only real difference is that now I can kick them out if they misbehave."

Tom chuckled.

"Actually, she uses us as deterrents," Michael declared. "Her swarms of men are easier to control with two big brothers in residence."

Annoyance lanced through Sarah. Really, she thought, sometimes Michael's sarcastic tongue was less than funny. Maybe she would raise his rent.

Jamie smiled. He recognized the truth of Michael's words, whether Sarah did or not. She carried her housemates along like shields. A funny combination of warmth and reserve was wee Sarah Hughes.

He admitted to himself that the paradox sparked his interest. Was that what drew him to her? he mused. Wondering what it would be like to breach the defenses and have all that warmth for his own?

The attraction to her was still growing, though he

14 · SUSAN RICHARDSON

was no closer to understanding it. As he looked at her, his stomach muscles tightened in arousal. He wanted her. And he was not feeling patient. He had to make a conscious effort to relax and take it slowly. He couldn't remember wanting a woman this much. He couldn't remember ever liking one so thoroughly and immediately.

They'd been driving through progressively woodsier streets for the last few minutes. Sarah finally pulled up the driveway of a long, low house surrounded by trees and a huge lawn. She felt, as always, a thrill of pleasure on coming home. This was hers—her place to come back to all her life. She'd never really had anything of her own before, and now she had this. She'd never leave it.

"Welcome to our house," she said to Jamie, smiling warmly.

The look on his face caused her to catch her breath. He was watching her with a brooding intensity that almost frightened her. This wasn't the warm, charming friend she thought she'd found. This was a powerful, perhaps ruthless stranger, and he was gazing at her like a predator at its prey.

In an instant he was smiling, and the dark impression faded. Sarah blinked and frowned, trying to decide whether or not she'd imagined it. Suddenly he winked and she almost jumped, she was so startled. It was as if he were saying, "I know what you're wondering, and wouldn't you like to know the answer."

Michael opened Sarah's door in an uncharacteristically chivalrous gesture and helped her out. He didn't like Sarah and Jamie gazing at each other with such intensity.

Sarah dug in her red canvas bag for her keys without really noticing what she was doing. She didn't know what to think. Sitting in the auditorium, watching and listening to Jamie, she'd felt she'd rediscovered something she'd been missing since the mother she'd adored had followed Sarah's father to a premature death. She knew this man would be important to her. Now, for the first time, it occurred to her that she really didn't know him at all.

Two

It was after midnight. Just a few late customers populated the bar. Jamie found a candlelit corner table, quite private. He installed Sarah gently in her seat, then went to get drinks for them.

He, Sarah, Tom, and Michael had had a pleasant hour at Sarah's, eating and listening to music in front of a fire, but more and more Sarah had watched Jamie and Jamie had watched Sarah. Sarah had been quite ready to leave by the time Jamie stood up and announced to Tom and Michael, "We're going for a wee walk, Sarah and I. You needn't wait up for us."

She laughed to herself as she heard Jamie insisting to the bartender that he wanted Scottish coffees. The Irish had stolen the idea, he claimed. Besides, they were much better with scotch whisky. He couldn't find it in his heart to drink the Irish stuff—felt it was unpatriotic.

He returned to the booth and plunked two steam-

FIDDLIN' FOOL • 17

ing glass mugs on the table. "Scottish coffees," he proclaimed triumphantly.

She smiled as she lifted her mug to her lips and blew gently on the cream. It was much too hot to drink yet. As she set it back down, she asked idly, "Are you always so Scottish?"

She realized as she said it that it could be taken as a criticism, though she hadn't meant it that way at all. She loved his Scottishness, though he did rather milk it.

He didn't take it as criticism. He smiled enigmatically as he sipped his drink, oblivious to its temperature. "It isn't all bogus, you know," he said mildly. "In fact, very little of it is. The corner of Scotland I come from is quite remote. The English spoken there is to this day a translation of the Gaelic."

He paused to move his mug thoughtfully in circles on the table. "Still," he added, tilting his head to look up at Sarah, "I must admit I've knocked around the globe enough to have my choice of idioms. I'm more Scottish when I've been away from home too long. Sort of a compensation, I suppose."

Her eyes widened in interest. "Tell me about your life," she said.

He shrugged deprecatingly. "I travel a lot. I play and listen to a lot of music. I try to let people know about traditional Scottish music. I'm organizing a festival of Celtic music to be held in Kentucky in midsummer, in fact."

He paused, then added, "I have some good friends all over the world, many of them musicians." He nodded, liking the sound of that. "Yes, you might say I'm part of a brotherhood of musicians. And that about sums it up."

It didn't, of course. Sarah knew there was a lot

18 • SUSAN RICHARDSON

more to Jamie McLeod than that, but she respected the boundaries he'd drawn. She knew how it felt to be questioned on sensitive subjects.

"Where were you before you came here?" she asked.

He smiled, remembering. "I've just spent a couple of weeks in Brittany. And before that I was in New York playing and studying for a month."

She shook her head in amazement. "A terribly hard life," she said ironically. "And where do you go from here?"

"Tomorrow I fly to Oregon for a concert, then to New Jersey for as long as it takes to record an album."

"Your life's nine-tenths excitement, isn't it?"

An enigmatic smile twisted his mouth. "Aye," he agreed blandly, "I'm just a happy-go-lucky fellow. A regular fiddlin' fool."

She stared at him, wondering why she kept getting the feeling he was leaving out more than he was putting in.

He met her assessing gaze. Swiftly he shot her a reassuring smile, then leaned across the small table toward her. "Try your drink now," he suggested, shoving her coffee toward her. "It'll warm you up and have you speaking the Gaelic yourself."

She cautiously sipped the beverage. Her eyes crinkled with her smile. "Mmm, good," she said.

He cupped his hands around his warm mug. "Tell me about yourself now," he said. "What do you do for a living, for instance?"

This was safe ground. Sarah loved talking about her work.

"I teach nursery school," she said, "and write children's books, mostly for older children—eight through twelve."

FIDDLIN' FOOL • 19

"Ah, and you use the little kiddies as raw material," he said, eyes twinkling. "Or is it all autobiographical, your work? Your own childhood experiences?"

At his teasing Sarah's face went from smiling to a bleak blankness so quickly, it was as if several frames of a film had been clumsily edited out. Jamie stared in astonishment. What had he said?

Bitter memories were passing through Sarah's mind. The black years. That was how she always thought of her life between the ages nine and eighteen. The years when she had been shuffled from foster home to foster home, never settling any one place, never wanted, it seemed, or wanted only halfheartedly, or for part of the time. She had had to learn how to handle rejection. She wouldn't have made it, otherwise. She'd built a wall to keep people from coming too close and relied only on herself. You were only vulnerable if you cared deeply, she had decided.

Autobiographical? No, her books were not autobiographical. Perhaps someday she'd write that story. But not yet. She wasn't far enough away from it.

Becoming aware that Jamie was watching her with deep compassion, she managed a travesty of a laugh. "No," she said, "my work isn't autobiographical. It's more fantasy than reality, actually. People like to read my stories because they let them live for a while in the world as it should be."

"And your childhood wasn't as it should be?" he asked gently. He was holding one of her hands between both of his own. She didn't remember his taking it.

For just a fraction of a second she considered

20 · SUSAN RICHARDSON

telling him just how imperfect her childhood had been. But the idea was dismissed as quickly as it had appeared. The slight tightening of her fingers around his before she slid her hand free was the only answer he got.

Her chin rose and her mouth firmed as she made herself meet Jamie's gaze. "There's no such thing as a perfect childhood, is there?" she asked. "Except in my stories," she added, softening the statement with a smile.

He smiled in turn, recognizing the evasion.

His slow, wise smile shook her. He knew she'd fobbed him off, and was letting it pass. And she knew he was more than capable of pinning her down if he wished.

This man wasn't going to be as easy to handle as most of those she met, Sarah realized. Just as with prospective parents, she had learned to keep men at a distance. It wasn't all that difficult, actually. A light touch here, the deft use of ridicule or a pretense of unawareness there. She had become very good at it.

So what was it about Jamie that threatened her defenses? She never thought about her childhood anymore, much less experienced the urge to tell anyone about it.

Jamie was still watching her carefully. Her color had returned, he noted in relief. He studied her face in the candlelight, delighting in the play of expressions over it, feeling a warmth deep in his chest.

I'm wondering about you very much, Sarah Hughes, he said silently. You are going to be a special lady for me.

It occurred to him that his object had shifted. He

FIDDLIN' FOOL • 21

no longer wanted only to get her into bed, though he was wanting that more as the evening wore on. He wanted to know her too—to unravel the mystery of her effect on him. To find out her history.

He was gazing at her mouth, fascinated by its shape. It was bare, free of lipstick or gloss, just smooth, tender curves. It moved him unbearably.

He reached out easily and slowly, and gently touched the corner of her lips, where there was a fleck of cream.

Shock jolted through Sarah and sped her heart into double time. Her hand was halfway to her lips, rising involuntarily before she caught herself and let it drop to her lap.

How did he do that? she asked herself wildly, her eyes wide. How did he do that to her with one finger? She'd never dreamed she could respond like that to a man.

"You have a very sexy mouth," he said, caressing it with his gaze. "I'd like to kiss it. For a long time."

Her own gaze flew to his firm lips, her mind filled suddenly with the idea of them pressed against her so. His mouth, which generally held amusement or irony, was now curved in a smile that was nothing if not sensual.

"And you," he added. "You'd like to kiss me too." His voice was very certain.

Little alarm bells went off in Sarah's head. She felt as if he were walking around in her mind. If he knew what she was thinking, she'd be lost. "I don't know that for sure," she said with a last attempt to deny what was unquestionably between them.

He lifted one shoulder impatiently. "Ach, yes, you do," he said, his tone holding a hint of disgust at

22 • *SUSAN RICHARDSON*

her evasion. "That you'd like to, that is. You just haven't made up your mind you're going to." He smiled wryly.

Sarah felt like a butterfly pinned to a board. "Well, I'm glad to see you're giving me a choice," she shot back tartly.

They weren't talking solely about kissing. That Sarah knew. They were talking about an attraction so strong that it was making her feel a little crazy.

He was right, of course. She did want him. Probably the signs were unmistakable, and he was undoubtedly experienced enough to read them.

But the idea of following through on a casual pickup—because that was what this was, right?—was too bizarre to contemplate. Wasn't it? Well, wasn't it? Her level-headed self was slow to answer.

Jamie sensed the struggle going on behind her blind gaze. What a fey woman she was, he thought. What had happened in her life to make her so cautious?

A powerful urge to comfort her ran through him. He gently took her hand, which was clenched around her mug, and turned it up to place his lips to her palm. Sarah's pulse raced. Her fingers curved instinctively to cup his face.

She looked down at Jamie's fair head bowed over her hand, and felt her heart turn over.

"Do you know," she said slowly, almost to herself, "I'm actually tempted. Isn't that odd?"

He lifted his head to stare intently into her face.

"It must be softening of the brain," she added. "I don't even know you."

He shook his head strongly. He wasn't buying that.

"Aye, you know me," he said, his voice almost stern. "We know each other, and on a deeper level than a cocktail-party introduction by mutual friends. If you deny that, it's disappointed I'll be in you."

She drew her hand from his, feeling defensive. "Ordinarily," she said, eyes flashing, "that sort of threat would be all it would take to have me denying it."

His lips twitched. He enjoyed her spirit and her honesty. He enjoyed prodding her. These American women were all so touchy about their independence.

And this one was touchy about other things as well. Give her a little space, man, he lectured himself. He tilted his chair onto its back legs and forced a patient smile onto his lips.

"Well, if it's more information you're needing," he said drolly, "let me tell you a bit about myself."

Sarah recognized the raconteur in his voice and settled back to be entertained. "All right," she said. "Do that."

He took a long swig of his drink in preparation, then began. "I'm clean, honest, and was brought up strictly." In an aside, he added, "I can't say the upbringing took, but the stock is good. I come from a close family. *They* all trust me."

This last was delivered with a reproachful look that drew an appreciative chuckle from Sarah.

He continued his enumeration. "I'm safe"—she doubted that—"not more than ordinarily kinky"—her gurgle of a laugh broke forth—"just a red-blooded, all-Scottish boy."

His endearing crooked grin tugged her own lips into a smile. She did love a man who could laugh at himself.

24 • SUSAN RICHARDSON

"I'm generally accounted a fairly accomplished lover," he went on. She could believe that, but she would rather not have heard it. "And I can offer you good, clean fun."

A pang struck Sarah in the region of her heart. She went still as she absorbed the blow. Well, she thought, that was honest. Good, clean fun. The attraction was no thunderbolt for him. She digested that in silence, running her finger around the rim of her mug. Wasn't it amazing, she marveled to herself, that even knowing he was casual about lovemaking, she was still tempted?

Jamie stared at her pale face, thinking it had been a foolish admission, perhaps, that bit about good, clean fun. But he'd never been one to mislead a woman. He refused to go into a relationship under false pretenses. And he also refused to let Sarah hide behind any comforting romantic illusions. If she came to him, it would be because they both frankly wanted and needed it.

He felt a little spurt of anger as a gadfly voice inside him asked, Who are you trying to convince, Jamie boy, her or yourself?

He shook his head to rid himself of the voice and continued with his pitch.

"Besides," he threw in teasingly, "I've nowhere else to stay."

She looked up at him from under her lashes. "You're not going to try to tell me your agent didn't book you a room," she said dryly.

Shamelessly, Jamie admitted, "I've already refused that one. It didn't meet my requirements."

Her mouth formed a soundless, mocking o. "Well," she said, unmoved, "there's a very nice motel not two blocks away."

FIDDLIN' FOOL • 25

Jamie tried hard to fill his voice with pathos. "You'd turn me away? A stranger in a strange land?"

"If you don't like the idea of a motel," she said heartlessly, "I'm sure with your line of patter you could charm your way into any number of other houses. That waitress over there, for instance"—she nodded toward a cheerful-looking redhead who'd been eyeing Jamie appreciatively since they'd come in—"would no doubt love to take you home."

Jamie didn't even turn his head. "But it's you I'm wanting, not a red-haired waitress."

Sarah grinned and he grinned back, fully aware that he'd admitted to noticing the waitress.

The bartender was making the rounds of the tables. "Closing time in fifteen minutes, folks," he announced.

Jamie nodded acknowledgment. "Right," he said without looking away from Sarah.

He leaned back in his chair, one hand in his pocket as the other lifted his mug to his lips. He took a sip, still challenging Sarah gently with his eyes. So you're going to remain pure and pretend this isn't happening? they taunted her.

She tossed her head in a gesture of defiance, but her smile somewhat spoiled the effect. It was his humor and his warmth that made it so difficult to snub him, she realized. His zaniness appealed too strongly to her own carefully repressed reckless streak.

Jamie was fighting a battle with his own impatience, a familiar battle. He wanted in the worst way to grab Sarah, to kiss her senseless, to force some admission of what he knew—that they were aching for each other, that this was meant to happen. Aye,

26 • SUSAN RICHARDSON

he thought, and said it again to himself, finding a surprising truth in it: She was for him.

He tossed his head back, draining his coffee. Needing to find some outlet for his impatience, he set the mug down on the table with an unnecessary bang.

Sarah's mouth curved in a smile. "That thump sounded very final," she said.

He smiled enigmatically, his eyes slitted and glinting in frustration. "Are you ready?" he asked.

She nodded. The coffee was really a bit strong for her. She'd happily leave the rest.

Outside the bar in the shadow of a tree, Jamie reached for her. Sarah put her arms around him and looked up at him, her eyes shining silver in the moonlight. A breeze blew a wisp of hair across her face. She ignored it, waiting patiently for his kiss. But patience turned to a trembling urgency as Jamie looked down at her broodingly.

She shouldn't be trusting him, he thought. He wasn't a safe person to be kissing in the moonlight, because he wouldn't settle for easy kisses and controlled passion.

He knew she expected a gentle, seductive kiss. But frustration and honesty drove him as he kissed her hard.

None of Sarah's previous limited experience with men had prepared her for the force of Jamie's kiss. She reeled under the impact of it. She seemed to lose her bearings and all point of contact with the earth as his firm mouth fastened on her soft one, pressing her lips against her teeth and arching her neck back.

Her hands clutched convulsively at his coat as a

sudden dizziness caught her. She was aware of nothing but warmth and power. Jamie's lips were warm; his body was a warm wall against hers; his strong hands on her back were warm. And his power surrounded her—not just the power of his body, but the strength of his character and his confidence.

The pounding of her blood echoed in her ears. Her lips parted and her body melted as Jamie lifted his head to stare at her with narrowed eyes.

Ah, now do you see? he asked her silently. Her eyes, smoky and opaque with desire, and her swollen mouth told him that she did. He wanted to leave her like that, with something to think about.

Her soft sigh caressed his face as her eyes slowly focused. Her hand slid up his chest to the back of his neck and stroked his hair.

With a groan Jamie abandoned the idea of stopping. He lowered his head and his mouth covered hers gently this time, though no less hungrily.

His arms pressed her to him more firmly, and he felt the yielding in her limbs. One hand slipped down to cup a slim hip; the other moved up to tangle itself in her hair. Her lips parted helplessly, and his tongue stroked and explored the inside of her mouth.

Heat rushed in a wild tide through Sarah. She moaned softly and moved obligingly to allow Jamie's hand the access to her breast that it was demanding.

Her breast was hot and round in his hand, the point begging for his touch as it pressed into his palm.

Did she know what she was doing? he wondered. Much more of this and she would feel committed, whether it was what she really wanted or not. Oh,

28 • SUSAN RICHARDSON

Lord, he thought in frustration, why did he have to have scruples?

He lifted his head reluctantly and watched her face as shock replaced blind hunger.

For Sarah, sanity returned in a rush. With a little thrill of fear she realized she had been badly out of control. That was not something she wanted to happen. She'd promised herself a hundred times as a child that she'd never again let her feelings make her vulnerable. Mindless passion was not for her.

Jamie puffed out his cheeks as he released an impatient sigh, then he put his hands on her shoulders and gently shook her from side to side. The gesture expressed his frustration more clearly than any words. She smiled in understanding. She felt frustrated, too, as well as alarmed.

He tucked her under his arm and set off down the street. Suddenly he lifted his head to the moon and howled, wolf-fashion. A laugh forced its way out of Sarah's tight throat, and she felt the tension drain out of her body.

She trusted him, she realized in surprise. She may have lost control, but he hadn't pressed his advantage. And instead of gloating, he'd just expressed his own frustration humorously. All his power had turned to taking care of her. A warmth filled her. This was quite a man.

They walked in silence. Their strides fit together surprisingly well, considering the difference in size. Sarah took two steps to every one of Jamie's, but still it felt right. His natural gait was slow and easy, and hers, quick and lively.

She felt curiously contented. She was quite happy not talking, and knew that Jamie was too. She enjoyed the night sounds. Distant sirens and the su-surration of cars passing on the busy streets behind them provided a background for nighttime rustlings in bushes and trees. The air smelled sweet.

Outside her back door, she reluctantly drew away from him to find her key. It felt so right next to him, it was an effort to move.

Behind her in the darkness, he said simply and devastatingly, "Will I stay the night?"

Three

Sarah bit her lip. Oh, dear. She had to make a decision, she realized. No more flirting with the possibilities.

She inserted her key in the lock and opened the door. The house was quiet and dim. Tom and Michael had gone to bed. She turned back to Jamie.

Very softly she said, "You're welcome to a place to sleep. There are several couches."

It was a decision, she supposed. Jamie accepted it as such. And he took it well. With a nod of acceptance, he said, "Good enough."

Sarah herself was finding it more difficult to live with her decision. Her mind had said no, but her body was clamoring to be heard. Say yes, it cried. Say yes.

Jamie leaned against a counter, facing her, his hands in his coat pockets. She leaned back against the opposite counter. Both their expressions were thoughtful, studying, smiles playing about their mouths.

FIDDLIN' FOOL • 31

Jamie was thinking that this was one of the harder things he'd done, this gentlemanly restraint. But she was fey. Pressuring her would be like strong-arming a dove.

Sarah was thinking that she couldn't make love with him, but she knew for sure she couldn't just say good night and walk off. She might never see him again.

After a minute of this mutual gazing, Jamie said, "I don't want to go to sleep just yet. Do you?"

She answered with a shake of her head.

"Tomorrow I catch a plane to Portland," he added, "and I'm not ready to say good-bye to you."

Uncanny that he should be thinking her thoughts, she mused. But she wasn't really surprised.

He did surprise her when he said, "Show me some of the books you've written."

She tilted her head questioningly. "You want a bedtime story?" she teased.

He smiled. "Maybe it will help me sleep."

"All right," she said. "I have copies back here." She led the way to her wing of the house—bedroom, bathroom, and tiny study. This had been the former owner's suite. Sarah had taken it for her own, loving the sense of privacy it gave her. Privacy was something she'd never had in the foster homes. And the fireplace in the bedroom was sheer luxury.

At the door to her small study, she stopped, feeling a sudden misgiving.

"It's a mess in here," she said hesitantly.

"Ah, then I particularly want to see it." The rest of the house was lovely. But he'd thought, looking at the glossy surfaces, "Where is Sarah in all this tidy decor?" He'd have expected cheerful litter, sentimental knickknacks. Over her shoulder he got a glimpse

32 • SUSAN RICHARDSON

of something bright in the room beyond. He reached past her to push the door open wider.

She shrugged and bit her lip as he stood in the doorway, surveying the room.

Aye, he thought. This was what he'd been looking for.

The study had the same white walls and polished hardwood floor as much of the rest of the house, but on the floor was also a colorful rag rug. The huge old oak desk and the sofa were scuffed and comfortable-looking—well loved and used.

On the desk was a scattering of papers and a typewriter with a piece of paper protruding from it. The walls were covered with photographs. Photos of smiling children, thoughtful children, swinging children, splashing children, shouting children, hugging children, sad children. Interspersed with the photos were drawings and paintings, crude shapes and bright colors with scrawled messages. *I love Sarha. Two Sarah. From Katie. Form Stephen.*

Some of the photographs included Sarah, and Jamie stepped into the room to look at these more closely. One in particular, a summertime picture, caught his eye. Sarah was hugging a small boy and being hugged fiercely back.

There was the Sarah he sensed, he thought. There were no barriers up here. Her face was radiant with love, almost painful in its vulnerability and compassion. He looked for a long time, until Sarah moved restlessly behind him.

"I can't seem to keep this room picked up," she said apologetically.

"And why should you, now?" he asked, turning a piercing gaze on her. "Who would want to box up what's in this room?" He sounded almost stern.

FIDDLIN' FOOL · 33

She smiled crookedly. She should know by now that she didn't need to make conventional noises at Jamie. "Yes," she said, acknowledging his perceptions, "this is my favorite room."

They smiled at each other in understanding.

Finding a row of books by Sarah on one of the shelves, Jamie selected several and settled himself on the sofa. Sarah sat in the desk chair. She idly pecked at the typewriter, adding a few words to the story she was working on. It didn't hold her attention, though. She turned instead to watch Jamie flip through her stories, thoroughly absorbed.

The V at the top of his shirt caught and held her attention. His neck looked strong, with its sinews and muscles, but smooth. Smooth and white. She'd never studied a man's Adam's apple before, but now she was fascinated by its protruberance and the hollow beneath it and between his collarbones. Her blood moved like molasses through her body, slow and heavily languorous. She forced herself to turn away. Even looking at him was dangerous.

Soon he shut the last of the books with a snap. She glanced over to see him smiling warmly at her. He said nothing, and she was grateful. The worst of having people read her books, she'd discovered, was knowing they felt they had to come up with appreciative, intelligent comments afterward. She should have realized Jamie would feel no such pressure. He responded less to other people's expectations than anyone she'd ever met.

Instead, he said, "Now show me your fiddle." She'd told him she dabbled.

She nibbled on her lower lip. "It's in the bedroom," she said reluctantly. It would have been a simple matter just to say, "I'll go get it," but some-

34 • SUSAN RICHARDSON

how that didn't occur to her at the moment. Her mind was preoccupied with thoughts of Jamie and the bedroom, and how firm was her decision to keep him out of there?

He threw up his hands in a protestation of innocence that his wicked grin belied. "Acquit me!" he said. "I didn't know. I'll wait just here. I'll not move my wee left toe. See? I'm a good boy."

Sarah suddenly felt foolish. And exasperated. And amused. All three emotions were becoming more and more familiar as the night wore on.

"Oh, all right, you Scottish clown," she said ungraciously, "come on then."

She flounced down the hall, not sure if she was more annoyed with him or with herself. She marched straight to her closet and flung open the door, then stooped to rummage among the shoes and boxes on the floor.

"It's in here," came her muffled voice from the depths.

Jamie smiled at the view of her bobbing jean-clad bottom as he undid the top button on his shirt.

Sarah emerged from the closet with her violin case and a face flushed from exertion and exasperation. Jamie was sitting on her bed removing his shoes. She raised her eyebrows.

He returned a bland smile, then stretched out on the double bed with a deep sigh, as at home as if he lived there.

Exasperation again turned to amusement. She opened her violin case and tuned the instrument. "What a restful man you are," she said ironically.

"Go on, say *lazy*," he challenged her, grinning as he crossed his arms behind his head. "You women are all alike. Never happy unless a man's leaping

FIDDLIN' FOOL • 35

around looking productive." She smiled at his outrageous exaggerations. "Well, I've done my hard work for the night. Now it's my turn to be entertained. Play for me."

She bowed in mock obedience. "Why does the word *laird* come to mind?" she asked innocently.

He waved a "lairdly" hand. "Play," he commanded imperiously, then lay back and closed his eyes.

Sarah complied, starting with "Soldier's Joy," a standard beginner's tune. Halfway through "Old Molly Hare," she noticed that the bed was shaking. Jamie had his arm over his face. She had thought he was concentrating on the music, but now it was clear he had another good reason to hide his face.

She stopped abruptly, hands on her hips in indignation, her violin in one, the bow in the other. "You beast," she said in hot indignation. "You asked me to play so that you could laugh at me!"

He shook his head vigorously in denial, but couldn't respond verbally because of the muffled, choking sounds fighting to come out of his mouth.

"You did!"

"No, no, I didn't, truly I didn't!" But this was less than convincing, as now howls of laughter poured out of him.

She put down her instrument and leaped on him, pummeling and shaking him. "You rude, horrible, tactless . . ."

He grabbed her hands to protect himself, still laughing helplessly. "Stop, stop," he begged.

"How would you like it if I'd sat snickering all through your concert?"

"As I recall," he replied, "you did begin the evening by grinning at me, as if you found something amusing about me." His mirth was under control

36 · SUSAN RICHARDSON

now, though it still crinkled his light blue eyes and drew creases in his cheeks.

He rolled so that she was beneath him and he lay halfway across her, still holding her wrists.

"And now that I bring it to mind," he said softly, with mock menace, "what was that all about?"

Her dimples came into play as she debated whether or not to tell him. He watched them come and go in fascination. Then he put a finger in a dimple, lightly caressing it.

Sarah went very still and her eyes grew huge. Her heart thumped almost painfully. She'd felt so close to Jamie, it had seemed perfectly natural to wrestle playfully with him. And now here she was underneath him on a bed. With no inclination to move.

He looked from her fading dimples to her mouth, which began to tremble slightly. "Eh?" he prompted, his gaze fixed on her lips.

Breathlessly, she said, "I was thinking you looked like a little boy of the giant species."

One brow rose. "Oh?" he said, drawing it out into a warning.

"Yes," she said, gazing at his thick, silvery pelt. "No grown man should have that kind of towhead. Or those eyelashes," she added, suddenly noticing how long and thick and fair they were. "You looked a bit like an enormous little boy." She was babbling. She knew she was babbling.

Jamie's clear blue gaze never left her face. He was studying her reactions like a scientist, not missing a thing. Her eyelids were quivering with apprehension. Something had made her cautious, he thought, and no mistake. Although she was nervous, it wasn't the stark panic she'd felt when she'd gotten carried away in their kiss earlier. Perhaps, if he were careful, he could someday erase her fear entirely.

"So I seem like a little boy, do I?" he asked with a slow smile.

A warmth was growing in the pit of Sarah's stomach. She couldn't keep it light any longer. She couldn't think of anything but how he was making her feel.

"No," she whispered with devastating honesty. "You're not a little boy." She was aching for him, and the risk didn't seem to matter any longer.

The feel of her body under his was doing drastic things to Jamie's blood pressure. She filled him with delight. Her humor, her spontaneity, her warmth. And now this complete honesty. Her eyes, that could cloud with hidden thoughts, were wide open now and clear.

He bent slowly to kiss her, watching desire flare in her smoky eyes and noting, too, the trace of fear with it.

His kiss was gentle, soothing. He held himself on a tight rein, though at the feel of those smooth warm lips beneath his, an urgency gripped his body. She was sweet. So sweet. He tasted her lips lightly once, then again. Her eyes closed and she breathed deeply, going with her desire. His tongue traced the outline of her lips and he felt her shudder.

The urgency took precedence. His tongue pressed against her teeth, and with a moan she gave him entrance.

Sarah felt as if she were being borne along on a tidal wave. There was no thought of resisting. She didn't want to resist. She surrendered all of herself, even her fear, into his keeping.

He felt the surrender, and he felt the fear. It was

38 · SUSAN RICHARDSON

enough. He could wait. He drew back and watched as her eyes slowly opened and even more slowly focused on his face. My Lord, he thought, what a gift of passion she would give. He wanted it all, without the reservations.

"Do you know what I thought when I first saw you?" he asked. She smiled, loving the sound of his deep, musical voice. Her body was still throbbing with arousal, but her breathing was uneven with her panic. She wasn't sorry to stop.

"What?" she asked, her own voice husky and not quite steady. " 'Why is that little twirp laughing at me?' "

"No. I thought you looked like a fallen angel, with that cloud of angel hair and your sexy, innocent face."

She bit her lip. Perhaps "falling angel" was more apt. Because she was falling. Not a doubt of that.

He ran his hands through her thick, fine golden curls. "Don't ever cut it," he ordered her, as if he had the right.

She smiled. "When I was a little girl, my mother used to say hair like mine couldn't be worn long. It's too thick and unruly. But I got tired of being called *cute*. Even *messy* was better. So I keep it long."

He looked at her provocatively. "But you're still cute," he teased. "As a button."

She reached for a pillow to throw at him.

He ducked his head. "Peace!" he called, intercepting the pillow. "That was simple justice, revenge for the towheaded-laddie remark."

She desisted, smiling at him. He shifted off her to lie at her side, head propped on his hand.

"I'm wanting very badly to make love to you, you

FIDDLIN' FOOL · 39

know," he said matter-of-factly, as if this were a piece of casual information that might interest her.

"I know," she said, grinning sassily. "Did you think you were keeping it secret?"

He smiled. "Do you know why I'm not going to?"

She looked indignant. "Because I don't want you to?" she asked huffily.

His own expression was gently admonishing. They both knew better than that. "Try again."

"Because you're too much of a gentleman," she said wickedly. He grinned. They both also knew better than that.

"Because when it happens," he said, "I want you to be as sure as I am that it's right."

He'd said *when*, not *if*, and he was smiling at her with total self-confidence. She should have resented it, she supposed, but instead she found it comforting. That meant there'd be another time, right?

"We'll see," she said softly.

She slid off the bed and set her violin and bow back in their case. She felt a restless need to move, to seek relief from the complex emotions churning in her.

"Aren't you going to play for me anymore?" Jamie asked, watching her with understanding in his eyes.

"When hell freezes over!" she said sweetly. Returning her violin case to the closet, she added, "I'm going to lock up the house."

Jamie lay back on the bed and closed his eyes. "Go ahead. I'm going to have a wee rest."

She smiled as she watched him sink into total immobility. He didn't look so threatening like this. Not at all like a tidal wave. Still enormous, of course, she thought, noting that his feet hung off the bed.

40 • SUSAN RICHARDSON

And still beautiful and powerful, with his chiseled features and perfectly proportioned limbs.

She stared at him for several minutes, indulging herself as he lay there with his eyes closed. In his motionlessness and with his fair skin and Viking-white hair, he could have been a statue. If she were a sculptor, she'd want to carve him. His face was a study in strength and humor.

Jamie knew what she was doing, of course, but self-consciousness was evidently not one of his problems. He opened an eye once, gave a little half-smile, then closed the eye. His breathing was deep and even, and soon he was asleep.

Sarah smiled and covered him with a blanket. He didn't budge. It was going to be her occupying the sofa bed in her study.

She locked the doors and lugged Jamie's duffel bag and fiddle into her bedroom. As she settled down for the night, she felt a surge of resentment that Jamie had just popped off to sleep so easily. Between relief and frustration, she knew she'd be awake for quite some time.

Four

Sarah awoke before Jamie the next morning. Probably musicians are used to late nights and sleeping in, she thought, peeking at him as she quietly collected her clothes. The white-blond stubble on his face was lighter than his skin. She could almost imagine what he would look like as an old man with a snowy beard. The thought made her smile and filled her with a tenderness so strong it shook her.

It was Friday, and Sarah herself didn't have the option of sleeping late. Sixteen bright and shining four-year-old faces would be turning expectantly toward her in little more than an hour.

She fastened her hair in a twist from which several curling wisps immediately escaped, then donned jeans and a bulky yellow sweater. Light colors weren't all that practical for nursery school, but she liked to be bright for the children.

She felt happy. As she sailed into the kitchen her "good morning" to her two housemates was almost a song.

42 • SUSAN RICHARDSON

They were nursing cups of coffee. Tom looked subdued. Michael looked downright surly. Oh, dear, Sarah thought.

Tom managed a good morning. Michael growled into his coffee.

"Our Scottish Lothario has departed the scene?" he asked in his usual sledgehammer manner.

Sarah's smile faded. They thought she and Jamie had slept together, she realized. Would they believe her if she told them they were wrong? On the other hand, they weren't all that far wrong. Besides, she thought with a lift of her chin, what business was it of theirs? Why should she have to justify herself to them? Her face took on a stern, unconscious dignity that had Michael figuratively backing up.

"Jamie McLeod," she said pointedly, "is still here and will be out shortly for breakfast. Any objections?"

"Dammit, Sarah—" Michael began, but Tom for once overruled him.

"No," he said firmly. "No objections." He quelled Michael with a look.

Sarah's eyebrows rose. Good for you, Tom, she thought. It was unusual and rather pleasant to see Tom drawing lines for his volatile friend.

"Fine," she said, smiling impishly at them. She wanted them to know she was fond of them even if she refused to allow comment on this area of her life.

"My turn to cook, isn't it?" she asked rhetorically, opening cupboards and rummaging for ingredients.

Tom nodded. Michael, needing to get in one parting, face-saving shot, grumbled, "If you're not too tired after your strenuous night."

She kept her back turned, so Michael didn't see her lips tighten. She was going to be very mature

FIDDLIN' FOOL • 43

and pretend he didn't say that, she told herself. But she wouldn't be surprised if she burned his breakfast.

Just thinking about it made her feel better.

She'd make pancakes this morning, with boysenberries and sour cream, she decided, just on the off chance that Jamie woke up before she left.

The yawning but freshly shaved and dressed object of her speculations appeared at that moment. "Good morning, all," he said pleasantly, noting and ignoring Michael's scowl and Tom's slight stiffness.

"I'm wondering if you can tell me how to connect up with a bus to the airport," he went on.

The housemates immediately brightened at the notion that Jamie would be departing shortly. He exchanged an amused glance with Sarah.

While she poured him a cup of coffee and went on with her cooking, he set himself to be pleasant to Tom and Michael. They were shortly over their snit, and by the time Sarah put breakfast in front of the three men, the atmosphere had changed completely. Laughter and animated conversation accompanied the food.

Jamie had pretty much ignored Sarah, concentrating on making the housemates like him. But Sarah, smiling and flipping pancakes, didn't mind. She felt his attention on her, even though it seemed to be directed to Tom and Michael. Just the way he touched her hand as she set the food in front of him was a conversation.

Michael looked at his watch in sudden consternation. "Oh, Lord, look at the time!" he said. He scraped his chair back and leaped for his jacket hanging over the back of another chair.

"Come on, Tom, I have to be on campus by eight-thirty." It was past that already.

44 • SUSAN RICHARDSON

The two men left in a flurry of farewells and exhortations to each other to hurry. Jamie calmly sipped his coffee.

Sarah smiled at him from where she stood behind the counter. "Your fascinating conversation had them too enthralled," she said dryly, knowing full well that he had exerted himself to be entertaining to the housemates.

He grinned wickedly. "If one wishes to see the princess, one must throw bones to the guard dogs."

"What a manipulative wretch you are!" she exclaimed, amused.

"Not at all." He rose to carry his coffee cup to the sink. "It's simple kindness to dumb animals. And basic strategy, of course."

"You're alarming me!" she said, not altogether in jest. There was that calculating, slightly ruthless streak in him that she'd noted before. She was very fond of Tom and Michael. Irritating as they frequently were, Michael especially, she wasn't positive she liked Jamie making fun of them.

He leered at her and twirled an imaginary mustache. "Heh, heh, heh," he chortled in old-fashioned melodrama style, "there's no escape for ye, ma pretty."

She smiled, then frowned. He was constantly doing it—reading her mind and making her feel foolish. She exhaled heavily and tried to look severe as he winked at her.

He poured a cup of coffee. "Here," he said, shoving it across the counter toward her. "You've been so busy waiting on the menfolk, you haven't had a mouthful."

She raised the cup to her lips.

"The pancakes were delicious," he said.

FIDDLIN' FOOL • 45

"Thank you." She watched in wonder as he rinsed the plates and began to load the dishwasher. "I *am* impressed," she said sincerely.

"Aye," he answered smugly, "I thought you would be. Humility and domesticity go over big these days. Does what 'treat 'em rough' used to."

She leaned against the counter. He had a lovely understated humor, she thought. Very dry and Scottish.

"Oh?" she asked. "You got good results in the old days with 'treat 'em rough'?"

"Not me. I was never very good at it. You have to have sincerity. I never could work up much enthusiasm for brutality."

He fit the last plate into its slot and reached for a hand towel. Drying his hands, he turned to smile broadly at Sarah. It was the first time they'd really focused on each other the entire morning.

Sarah liked that. She liked knowing that whatever Jamie did would be what he felt like doing, not what some romantic convention or expectation told him to do. Nor did she need whispers and sighs and burning looks. She needed him just the way he was. Totally himself.

"I suppose you have to go to work?" he asked wistfully.

She nodded.

"You wouldn't like to chuck all that and come to bed with me? We've known each other almost a day now, so the unseemly-haste factor is gone."

She shook her head gently as warmth flooded her body.

He sighed. "I thought not," he said, then just looked at her for a long moment.

"Sarah, Sarah," he murmured at last, almost as if

46 • SUSAN RICHARDSON

he were scolding her. He shook his head, seemingly in disbelief.

She smiled. "What?" she asked.

"Just 'Sarah,' It's the first line of a new song I'm writing. I'll play it for you someday."

That was enough of a promise for her. Her smile grew wobbly around the edges as they looked at each other.

"I have to go," she said reluctantly. "You're welcome to stay here as long as you like."

"No, I'll make my way to the airport. My agent would flay me if I missed this concert in Portland. He's spent months arranging it."

Again, it was ordinary conversation. But their eyes never left each other's, and their smiles never faded.

At last Jamie held out his hand. Sarah took it and they walked together to her room to collect her shoulder bag and his fiddle and duffel bag.

They strolled to her car like that, holding hands but not speaking.

"Can I drop you someplace?" she asked. "The bus station?"

"No," he said. "I'm used to making my own way."

"All right." She stood on tiptoe to touch her lips to his. He barely responded, and his hands stayed at his sides. But his eyes were devouring her.

They both sighed, almost at the same moment.

"See you," he said finally.

She nodded.

She watched as he strode to the end of the block. Before he rounded the corner, he turned back to her. He made no sign, didn't wave or nod. Just looked for a moment, then walked on out of sight.

Scraps of an old song about a rolling stone gathering no moss played through Sarah's head.

FIDDLIN' FOOL • 47

She felt as if the sun had gone behind a dark cloud. It had been all she could do at the last to keep from clutching him and begging, "Please don't go. Please stay with me. It's been so lonely without you." But, as always, pride had held her up. She had stood alone and independent . . . and watched him go. Depression settled over her like a thick fog rolling off the ocean.

The morning at school was all right on the surface. The children were a bit more clinging than usual, as they always were when they sensed something amiss with the important adults in their lives.

Sarah held them close, as much for her own sake as for theirs. She could use a little cuddling, she told herself. She felt cold.

Getting through the morning was like wading through molasses. Her every movement had to be thought out because all her energy was channeled into flashes of memory and the effort required to suppress the emotions they brought forth.

Little Maggie Owens, running gleefully out the door and into the play yard, tripped. Joy turned to anguish in an instant. "My toe!" she wailed, hurling herself at Sarah in passionate dismay.

Holding Maggie and soothing her, Sarah remembered how it felt to be like Maggie. Every feeling flying and the total faith that a loving adult would welcome the chance to heal your hurts.

And she remembered feeling very different when she was ten and had realized that love and sympathetic understanding were not a birthright.

She looked around at the bright, happy, independent children and thought of the first group of little ones she'd had charge of. It was with Tass, the

48 · SUSAN RICHARDSON

preoccupied, vaguely kind woman who'd fostered Sarah during her last two high-school years. Tass had done day care for children ages two through six, and she'd openly exploited Sarah's services every afternoon. Sarah hadn't minded, though. She adored children and they adored her. With children she came the closest to recapturing the warmth and happiness of her own early childhood. And to give Tass her due, she had paid Sarah.

The children had been from low-income or no-income homes, where life was not easy and few of them got or expected much attention from their overworked parents. Sarah's offers of affection had been met either with suspicion or frantic clinging. She'd realized then that no matter how drab her life had become, she'd had a priceless beginning. She'd sworn that no child she ever came in contact with would lack for love and laughter.

She'd stopped looking for it herself, though, until Jamie McLeod had offered it to her. And taken it away with him.

Somehow, the morning ended. Thank goodness the job was only part-time, Sarah thought as she climbed into her car at the end of the session. She couldn't have carried it off much longer. Every muscle in her face and body ached from the strain of keeping grief and memories at bay.

Alone in her own house finally, she locked the door to her wing, lowered the wooden window shades, and curled up in a chair. She couldn't fight them any longer, so she let the memories, and the tears, come.

She remembered the golden years, when her parents were alive. And the black years in various foster homes.

During the bad times something had hardened in Sarah, so that she no longer counted on anyone for anything. She'd known her life was hers to make what she could of it. No loving parent would ever take care of things for her. So she'd saved and studied. She'd earned a scholarship to one of the best universities in the country, and when she'd gone there, she never looked back.

She had friends, good ones. She had boyfriends— carefully chosen, thoughtful men. She'd convinced herself she was serious about one once, and had even slept with him, just to prove to herself that she was a whole woman. To her surprise, she had found sex quite pleasant. It was never more than that, though. She had too many guards up.

She hadn't slept with Jamie, but she knew that it would have been more than "quite pleasant" with him; it would have been making love. He would have swept all her guards away, partly with his sheer physical charisma, partly with that quality of irreverent joy that was so like the sunny zest her own parents had possessed. Sarah was always the charmer in her circles, the one who provided the spark, the zip. Until Jamie, she'd met no one who was in her class for verve. In him, though, was the quality of joyous living she'd been missing since her parents had died. He brought her to life. And it hurt.

"Damn you, Jamie McLeod!" she whispered to her knees, where her head rested. "I was fine as I was. Now look at me!"

At the words, Sarah's perspective suddenly shifted, as if something had shaken the kaleidoscope of her brain, and she did look at herself. She saw a grown woman sitting in a darkened room indulging in a fit

50 · SUSAN RICHARDSON

of the utter dismals, and a watery chuckle escaped her. This was not her usual style.

She slowly unfurled herself and straightened. Her face felt stiff from the tears that had dried on it, but the aching strain that came from holding in her emotions was gone. She breathed slowly and deeply, watching the play of dust motes in the slits of light that sliced in between the slats of the wooden blinds. A kind of peace came over her.

She might damn Jamie McLeod, but she knew that the grief he'd triggered had been occupying space in her heart for too long. Even if she had to feel grief to feel again at all, perhaps it would be worth it. Perhaps she was ready to trust life again.

And perhaps she had no choice. The process that had begun the instant she'd set eyes on Jamie McLeod showed no signs of stopping.

She might decide rationally that Jamie was a learning experience, Sarah thought wryly a week later as she cuddled a cup of coffee at six in the morning, but her body had its own ideas. It thought Jamie should be there with her, and it refused to sleep if he wasn't.

She'd gotten up and made coffee, tired of trying to force sleep.

Michael wandered into the kitchen, stretching and yawning. "What are you doing up?" he asked in surprise. He was the early riser around the house. Sarah usually slept as late as possible.

"Couldn't sleep," she replied laconically. "Want some coffee? It's fresh."

He nodded, and she poured as he pulled a stool up to the counter.

"How long can this go on?" he asked truculently, eyeing the circles under her eyes and her listless posture. "You look like hell!"

She sighed wearily. "Michael, do me a favor. Don't say 'I told you so.' "

They glared at each other for a moment, until the scene began to seem funny to Sarah. She smiled, and Michael slowly followed suit.

"Well, I don't have to, do I?" he said gently. They sipped in companionable silence for a minute. "I just hate to see you like this, Sarah," he added.

She patted his hand. "I know, and thanks for your concern. But it can't last forever, can it? And it's my own stupid fault."

Michael carefully refrained from comment, but the expression on his face agreed with her.

She gave a short laugh. "What a predicament! Careful, self-respecting me besotted with a musical Johnny who's probably forgotten my name."

Michael shook his head and stared into his coffee cup, sharing her disbelief.

"Ah, well," she continued, "at least now I know what all that can't-sleep, can't-eat, lovesick stuff is about. That's always useful for a writer. I never understood how anyone could be so stupid, before." She often rationalized pain this way. Now she could write about it convincingly. Good. That was helpful.

Michael offered his brand of consolation. "Eveyone's entitled to make a fool of themselves once."

She slanted him an amused look. He was making her feel better, not with kindly reassurances, but because his attempts at cheering her up were so funny.

"Well," she said, "it doesn't look like I'll get the chance to go for twice."

52 · SUSAN RICHARDSON

He cleared his throat uncomfortably. "Did you see his picture in last night's paper?" he asked.

"Yes, I saw it," she said wearily.

Jamie had been smiling at an extremely glamorous Hollywood actress who was wearing a slinky dress. He'd looked much as he had here, in a tweed jacket and jeans, his fiddle tucked under his arm. The caption had read, "THE FIDDLER AND THE FLAME. In New York sultry Helen Marlin discusses film collaboration with musician Jamie McLeod."

Sarah had burned with humiliation. That she had thought she was something special to Jamie McLeod, who chatted with famous beauties daily, seemed ludicrous. She felt like the original country bumpkin.

The phone rang and she reached for it in surprise. Who would call at six in the morning?

"Hello?"

"Have you practiced your fiddle today?" the deep, musical voice asked. "I'm expecting to see no little improvement, you know."

Sarah felt as if she'd been dropped from a great height. Hope and delight flooded her body.

"Jamie!" she breathed. The misgivings of the moment before evaporated magically.

Michael groaned and rolled his eyes. Shaking his head and muttering "This I refuse to watch," he left the room.

"Where are you?" Sarah was saying into the phone.

"Not where I'd like to be," Jamie said. "I'm in New Jersey, slaving day and night in a stuffy rehearsal studio to satisfy the most exacting producer it's ever been my misfortune to encounter."

His voice had gathered strength and indignation as the sentence progressed. It was a heartfelt complaint.

She chuckled. "Yes, you stars of the entertainment world have a hard time, I've heard."

FIDDLIN' FOOL · 53

He snorted. "The only stars in this business are the managers and producers. I'm just a workhorse."

"Poor Jamie," she said with amusement.

"Aye, you can mock, out there romping through the California poppies like a pied piperess with sixteen glowing children in train. You have no idea how I yearn for the open country."

"Poor Jamie," she said again, this time sincerely. There was no mistaking the wistfulness in his voice. "You're welcome to come visit and romp in the fields with us any time, you know."

"I may just do that," he said softly. "And before so very long too."

Her heart jerked with happiness. She squeezed the phone tightly for a moment before she could speak again.

"The recording is going well?" she asked finally.

"Aye. Between takes I'm working on the new song I started with you. I hope to have it in shape in time to record on this album."

"Oh?" she said weakly, remembering that he'd said "Sarah" was the first word in his new song.

"Yes. I'm going to call it 'Unseemly Haste.' "

She laughed, sure now that they were discussing the same song.

"I wanted to call it 'Ode to Sarah's Body,' " he continued in his dry, humorous voice, "but the producer wouldn't go for that."

"Jamie!" she protested weakly.

"It was going to be the first in a series, followed by 'Ode to Sarah's Voice,' 'Ode to Sarah's Eyebrows,' and so on."

She chuckled. "Yes, well, I've started a new book too. It's called *The Towheaded Laddie*."

"That sounds very exciting," he said approvingly. "But are you sure it's suitable for children?"

54 · SUSAN RICHARDSON

"It will have to be carefully edited," she agreed, smiling into the phone.

He chuckled, then they both fell silent for a moment. Sarah was fighting herself to keep from asking when she would see him.

His voice came clearly across the line, sharper than before. "Sarah," he said intently. Then nothing.

"Yes?" she prompted.

He sighed in obvious frustration. "Nothing," he said slowly.

She bit her lip. She wanted him to say what he had been about to.

Instead, he said, "Take care of yourself, will you?"

"I will. You do the same."

"Bye-bye, just now," he said, very Scottish, and hung up.

Sarah sat holding the phone for a moment, a potent mixture of happiness and yearning sweeping over her. She would see him again. She knew she would. But could she wait? If she'd known where he was recording, she wouldn't have trusted herself not to catch a plane.

She slowly replaced the receiver on its hook and hugged herself tightly. Before she'd barely had the energy to drag herself around, and now exhilaration was bubbling in her veins.

She hurried into the living room to put on one of Jamie's records, needing to have something of him with her. As she examined a record, she realized she'd have to buy some new ones. These were getting somewhat worn.

Five

Six days later Jamie sat in the darkness of Sarah's kitchen. His chair was tipped onto its back legs. One hand was shoved deep into his pants pocket, the other drummed impatiently on the table. He could have turned the lights on, but there was nothing he wanted to see that was there.

Sarah wasn't there. He had arrived about ten that night, on fire to see her, only to find the house dark and empty. Getting in had presented no problem. Sarah had left the back door open. He wanted to scold her for that, and the fact that he couldn't because she wasn't there increased his impatience.

For two hours he'd been sitting there, his gaze fixed on the front porch, which he could see through the living room window from where he sat. Where the hell was she? It was midnight, for pity's sake. He knew he was being irrational—she did have a life of her own—but he couldn't talk himself out of it.

He'd worked like a fool to finish his recording session, taking time out only to eat, sleep, and call

55

56 • SUSAN RICHARDSON

Sarah nearly every day. He'd spent most of this day at Newark Airport, waiting for space to come available on a San Francisco flight. He'd tried to call Sarah to tell her he was coming, but hadn't been able to reach her. Why he had expected her to be waiting to greet him with open arms anyway he didn't know, but he had. He wanted to smash something.

Finally he stood up, scraping his chair across the floor with violent irritation, and strode to the cupboard where he remembered Sarah kept the glasses. Rummaging in the refrigerator, he found an open bottle of white wine. He poured himself a glass, then carried it and the bottle back to the table to resume his vigil, impatience growing to rage within him.

He didn't have to wait much longer. At twelve-twenty a car pulled up in front of the house. He heard doors slam, then a man's cheerful voice and Sarah's rippling laugh, growing louder as they approached the front door. If she brought him in, Jamie swore silently, he'd kill him.

They stepped onto the porch and he could see Sarah search in her bag for her keys. Why bother? he thought sourly. The house was wide open. In his present mood he was ready to carp at anything.

She had her back to him. She was wearing a pair of red slacks, and the shape they outlined had his blood stirring. Paradoxically, the sensation fueled his anger.

As he watched, Sarah's date put his arms around her and pulled her to him. She lifted her face to his and sweetly kissed him good night. Jamie's grip on the wineglass tightened until the stem snapped. He didn't even notice that his fingers were cut. His gaze

FIDDLIN' FOOL • 57

never moved from the pair on the porch. Only his flaring nostrils and glittering eyes showed emotion.

Sarah pulled back. He saw her smile and heard her say, "Good night, Mark. I had a good time."

Mark murmured something Jamie didn't catch and lowered his head again to kiss her. Jamie half-rose from his seat, but Sarah had turned away to insert her key in the door. It was nicely done, Jamie noted as he settled back into his chair, leaving Mark thinking she hadn't noticed his overture and so hadn't rejected it. She'd evidently had a good deal of practice in holding men at arm's length.

As the door swung open, Sarah softly said good night again and slipped inside. Mark walked off to his car, whistling and no doubt feeling very fine. Jamie felt like hell.

Sarah switched on a light, then turned and saw Jamie. She gasped, startled at first to find someone sitting in her kitchen. She recovered quickly, though, her joy overcoming her momentary fright.

"Jamie!" she cried, every bit of her reaching out to him in welcome. Dropping her bag on the floor, she flew across the room to hurl herself at him. "I'm so glad to see you!" she exclaimed.

Sitting on his lap with her arms around his neck, she finally realized that he was not reciprocating her greeting.

She pulled back slightly to look at his grim face and hard eyes. "What's the matter?" she asked in surprise.

He glared at her with something akin to dislike. "I don't like you kissing other men," he said between clenched teeth, his accent at its most Scottish.

She gave a little incredulous laugh, thinking he

58 • SUSAN RICHARDSON

was teasing. When his expression didn't change, her smile faded into puzzlement.

"Am I supposed to just drop all my friends now that I've met you?" she asked reasonably.

"Just all your lovers," he shot back. He hated this. He hated being put in the position of the jealous lover. He felt ridiculous. But he couldn't stop himself.

And if an attractive old female friend had presented herself one night last week, he asked himself, would he have told her to move on? The answer to that scared him. Yes, he would have! He didn't want anyone but Sarah. The realization of what that might mean made him feel more stubborn and angry. His jaw jutted out aggressively.

Sarah stared at him pensively. He was really angry, she thought. She supposed she should worry, but she couldn't help being a bit pleased that he was jealous. She must mean something to him.

"Mark's not a lover," she said, thinking to placate Jamie.

His fist suddenly pounded the table, making her jump.

"Then why were you kissing him?" he asked harshly.

He was *really* angry, Sarah realized. This was no joke. She didn't want him this angry at her. She didn't want to play games with him.

She stroked his face and leaned against his chest. "Let's not argue," she pleaded. "I'm so glad to see you. I'm probably a fool for admitting this—and for letting it happen—but you're the only man I really want to kiss."

She waited for him to relax, to relent, but his expression remained frozen. There was a far-off look in his eyes. She bit her lip, not sure what to do to

FIDDLIN' FOOL • 59

bring him back. This was the side of him she'd glimpsed in the car that first night—the powerful, ruthless stranger. She wanted the warm, witty, loving man back.

Jamie was caught up in amazement at his reactions. Something primitive was moving in him. He wanted to kill these other men. He wanted it clearly understood that anyone who touched his woman would die. This was no mere jealous fit. It was something much more profound.

"Jamie?" Sarah asked softly. Then she noticed the blood on his fingers. "Jamie!" she said in a different voice. "You've cut yourself!"

He looked down at the drying blood on his fingers. "So I have," he said without interest.

"Let me get something for—" she began, but he held her when she would have risen.

"No, it's nothing," he said. "Stay here."

Finally he looked at her as if he really saw her. He was frowning still, but he was there, Sarah knew, with her.

His jaw clenched as he pulled her head to his. She went gladly where he guided her. His kiss held a hint of anger—certainly it was the dominant urge within him—but she responded with her whole soul. With a groan he gathered her close, burying his face in her neck.

He spoke against her throat, and his words sounded as if they'd been wrenched from him. "I've missed you."

Her heart sang. That was a serious admission for this rolling stone, she felt. And one not easily made.

"I've missed you too," she told him from her heart.

He raised his head and looked straight at her. He

60 • SUSAN RICHARDSON

was no longer frowning, but he still wasn't smiling, not by a long shot. She wanted to see him smile.

"The way you were talking," she said, tongue well in cheek, "I thought you were considering killing Mark and confiscating all his cattle."

A wry half-smile appeared on his face. He knew she was joking and had no idea how close that was to the truth.

"Aye, we're all barbarians, we Scots," he agreed.

She smiled, delighted to have him revert to playing on his Scottishness. Anything to lift that bleak look from his eyes.

He was watching her. He had a way of looking at her that made her feel most other people never truly saw her. Jamie really looked. He studied her, seeming to absorb everything her face had to tell. She watched him in turn.

"We're going to the bedroom," he announced. "Would you like me to carry you, barbarian fashion, or shall we walk?"

Her gamin grin flashed across her face. "Oh, barbarian fashion, without doubt," she said definitely. She wasn't arguing. They both knew the only question was *how* they were going, not if they were.

At last the real Jamie McLeod appeared as he laughed at her choice. "Very well," he said, standing up with her in his arms. "I'm an exhausted man, but I will not let my stereotypes down."

"Good," she said. "I do like consistency in a man."

"Consistency you shall have," he said, his voice promising more than the words indicated.

He strode down the hall to Sarah's wing and kicked the door open. Instead of heading for the bedroom, though, he carried her into the bathroom.

"What are we doing in here?" she asked, her eyebrows raised.

"Just a wee detour," he said, as if that were a reasonable explanation. Still holding her, he sat on the edge of the tub and turned on the water. "I've been traveling all day. I wouldn't ask a dog to sleep with me as I am."

That was half the truth. He didn't tell Sarah the real reason they were here, which was that another man had just kissed her good night. He could smell aftershave on her. He'd make love to her, but first he'd eradicate every trace of that man. From her body, and from her mind.

She laughed. "You're insane, do you know that?"

"Totally mad," he agreed. "It's a well-known fact." He grinned at her as he adjusted the temperature of the water and switched the flow to the shower head. Then he stood and lowered her carefully to the floor, focusing all his attention on her. He ran his fingers lingeringly through her hair. His anger was fading and his hunger growing.

She looked up at him, and her breath caught in her throat at the glow in his eyes. The inclination to joke fled. When he looked at her like that, she felt she'd follow him into a closet.

"Do you want me to wait in the other room?" she asked breathlessly.

He shook his head, smiling crookedly. She was going nowhere. He wasn't risking the return of her cautiousness. "You're coming in with me," he informed her. "I'm a very fastidious fellow. I'll need you to scrub my back."

The words were light; the tone was not. Sarah's eyes grew wide and her knees weak.

He smiled and lifted a hand to the buttons of her

62 • SUSAN RICHARDSON

shirt. She watched his face as his fingers worked their way down to her waist. "I must be out of my mind," she whispered, almost to herself.

His smile grew. "Aye, we're mad together." He caressed her throat with his mouth as his hands slipped inside her shirt and around her back to unfasten her lacy bra.

Her eyes closed and her head fell back. The sound of the shower was suddenly very loud, masking the heaviness of her breathing. Shirt and bra fell from her shoulders. As sensation claimed her, she wondered idly if Jamie would find her beautiful. She wanted to see pleasure in his eyes when he looked at her.

She gazed at him and saw his appreciative smile as he gently cupped one breast. Then he shook his head and quickly slid the rest of her clothes down over her hips and off her.

"Be with you in a second," he said as he held the shower curtain aside for her. His voice wasn't completely steady.

She obligingly stepped into the tub, feeling as if she were moving in a dream.

The curtain fell between them, and Sarah closed her eyes, letting the warm water beat on her face and head and plaster her hair to her neck and shoulders. She shivered and wondered if it was with anticipation or apprehension.

As Jamie quickly stripped, he studied her through the transparent shower curtain. She stood straight and slender, her rapt face raised to the spray. Water cascaded over her, flowing in streams around her small, shapely breasts. For a moment he stood and looked his fill. If Sarah had seen his expression, she might have had some doubts, for it held as much pain as pleasure.

What a thing of beauty she was, he thought. The line from her throat to the point of her breast was a poem; the shape of her flank a melody. He would write a song to her body, see if he wouldn't.

He held back the shower curtain to step between her and the stream of water.

Sarah opened her eyes. An enormous expanse of muscled white flesh filled her field of vision. She smiled at him. "Hello," she said dreamily, still floating on the currents that flowed between them.

His soaked hair was a dark silver. Water poured over his shoulders and down the front of him in sheets. She put her hands out and splayed them on his chest, watching the sheets break up into rivulets, loving the hard warmth of him.

His own hands pressed against her back, bringing her close to him. A shudder passed through her body. The tidal wave was back, threatening to overwhelm her. Jamie's sheer maleness beat at her senses; his size and strength enveloped her.

Jamie watched her eyes widen, then feather closed, recognizing her reaction. What had happened in her life, he wondered, to put that fear in her? An inept lover? A rigid upbringing? Someday, he promised himself, he'd know all there was to know about wee Sarah Hughes. For now, he'd take it slowly. He didn't want to lose her.

Her eyes fluttered open again when she heard his voice, surprisingly light. "Where's the soap?" he asked.

The ordinariness of that, in the midst of this momentous scene, was somehow reassuring, and Sarah

64 • SUSAN RICHARDSON

laughed. He'd put that somewhere in the song, too, Jamie thought.

"If you'd given me advance notice," she said teasingly, "I'd have stocked your brand."

"I'm fastidious, but not particular," he said. His arms tightened around her. The hunger was getting stronger.

Sarah was feeling weaker by the second. Jamie was so very large and so completely at home in this situation. He evidently had no self-consciousness about bodies. He studied her with deep appreciation, and she somehow knew he could march naked down Wall Street without blinking.

She slid her hands up to his shoulders, then down over his biceps to his elbows, memorizing the shapes of him.

"Such a gargantuan thing you are," she said, wanting to postpone the moment when the waves crashed over her. "Where did you get these bulges here? Throwing logs, or whatever barbaric thing it is you wild Scotsmen do?"

"Please," he said reprovingly, "the caber. I toss the caber. Scottish Games champion three years running. It drives the lassies wild. Just mention that you're a Games champion and they're lined up in the heather three deep. Are you duly impressed?" The grooves in his cheeks were clearly in evidence, his eyes twinkling roguishly.

Sarah smiled. She doubted he'd ever been within three feet of a caber. She also had no doubt that he'd throw it well, whatever it was, if he did get near one. He had that kind of competence about him.

"Oh, duly," she said teasingly, trying to hide from him and from herself just how impressed she was.

She reached for the soap and lathered her hands.

FIDDLIN' FOOL • 65

Jamie took the cake from her and soaped his own large paws. He smoothed the lather over her shoulders and arms.

"You've a fine small set of muscles yourself," he said. "What do you do to keep in such very fine shape?"

The air was thickening with steamy vapor, and Sarah was finding it increasingly difficult to breathe. Jamie held her in the crook of one arm while his other hand soaped her. His voice was matter-of-fact, casual; his expression friendly and warm. She believed she was holding up her end of the conversation, but it was getting harder to keep her mind on his words.

He was paying careful attention to her breasts now, and she thought she might literally faint. If he weren't holding her up, she might fall.

"These days I sprint after the children," she answered in a small voice, "but I went through college on a gymnastics scholarship."

"Ah, that explains it," he said, his voice wrapping her in velvet. "You're just a wee bit thing. But all of it perfect."

Since she seemed incapable of speech, he continued. "Gymnastics. Isn't that where you contort yourself into impossible positions?"

His hands moved from her tight, swollen breasts to her stomach. He carefully soaped each hip and explored the flat, quivering space between. A low moan escaped from Sarah's parted lips.

He caressed the triangle between her legs, and her head fell back as warmth flowed through her. All her muscles seemed to have gone slack. As she listened to him, her body was free to go its own way, or rather, Jamie's way. He was taking her deeper and

66 • SUSAN RICHARDSON

deeper into a realm of sensuality she'd never dreamed of, while his voice lulled her with its cheerful teasing.

"You'll have to give me a gymnastics demonstration sometime."

She murmured something unintelligible as he pressed her to him, their bodies touching from breast to knee, and ran talented hands down her back.

"Yes," the amused, audacious voice went on, "that could make for interesting possibilities. You'll be a very flexible lover."

A gusty little laugh whispered out of Sarah, but she was incapable of speech. And he'd teased her long enough. Her body craved the feel of his.

She reached behind his head and brought his face down to hers, her mouth opening in full invitation, hot and moist.

It was what he'd been waiting for. She was ready now to make her own demands. He wrapped his arms lightly around her as he kissed her thoroughly.

When he lifted his head to speak, the spellbinding voice was gone. He spoke intimately and urgently.

"I don't want to stop," he said. "I want to take you here. The bed will have to wait."

In answer, she stretched on tiptoe to fit herself to him. "Yes," she said simply.

A strangled laugh forced itself out of Jamie's throat. His hands cupped her buttocks to lift her into position and his mouth found hers again.

Sarah wrapped her arms and legs around him and abandoned herself to the waves of ecstasy that crashed over her. Water beat on her back, on her face. The roaring in her ears and her blood rivaled the elemental force of a tsunami. She was buffeted and hurled from one ocean peak to another. And through it all she clung to Jamie. He was the center of the storm. He was sea centaur and merman. With him she was safe, in the depths or riding the foam-curled crests.

She buried her face in his neck and tasted warm skin and warm water. As her universe dissolved she heard Jamie's hoarse shout, "Sarah! My God, Sarah!"

Later Sarah would wonder how Jamie kept his footing in the slippery tub under the weight of the two of them. But at the time she knew that he wouldn't let her fall. She was secure in his hands. She gave everything she had to give and received everything there was to receive. She hadn't known. She really had had no idea such self-obliterating exhilaration existed.

They clung together on the floor of the tub, where they'd sunk at last, neither of them capable of standing upright. Jamie was drawing breath into his lungs in deep gulps. Sarah was panting, trying to slow her breathing.

"I'm drowning," she said in comic dismay. "I can't move, and I'm drowning."

His rumbling laughter sounded breathless. "I know." He reached behind him and turned off the water. "We'll still drown," he said, "just breathing this waterlogged air."

They both chuckled helplessly. Jamie seemed to gather his strength, then he heaved himself to his feet. "Come on," he said.

He dragged Sarah to her feet, and she swayed while he reached for a towel. "Hold still," he commanded her. "You're as slippery as a trout."

She choked on a laugh. "How romantic," she

68 • SUSAN RICHARDSON

said without heat. "The fun's over, no more sweet phrases?"

He grinned, completely unrepentant, as he wrapped her in a towel. He swung her unsteadily up into his arms and lurched out of the tub. They were both laughing uncontrollably.

"I know now where that story about Delilah originated," he said. "I can hardly move."

Sarah, expending no effort at all as poor Jamie staggered into the bedroom, said, "You should have consair-r-rved your strength," mocking his beautiful accent.

She squeaked as he dumped her unceremoniously on the bed and fell beside her. "The flight was lovely, but the landing was a bit rough," she murmured as he dragged the covers up over the two of them.

"Shut up," he said kindly, gathering her to him and closing his eyes.

She snuggled against him, fitting her body to his, as comfortable as a kitten. Contentment and a sense of wonder filled her.

They were both asleep within minutes.

Six

Sometime later, Sarah surfaced from a dreamless sleep, gradually becoming aware of Jamie's quiet, efficient movements as he set about making a fire. The room was in darkness except for the faint but growing glow from the fireplace.

She propped herself up on one elbow to watch him, holding the covers to her chest to keep warm. Jamie didn't seem to feel the cold. At least he'd felt no need to cover himself. His hard-muscled body gleamed like alabaster in the firelight. He was all ice and snow, she thought, strange for such a warm, sunny-tempered, earthy person.

She mused about stereotypes, thinking the whiteness of Jamie's skin could be used in ads for suntan lotion as a pitiful contrast to the deep tan of the star model. Pale flesh was puny, unmanly, a sign of a sedentary indoor life, the advertisement would suggest. Real men took their shirts off while performing hard physical labor in the sunshine.

She smiled to herself. No one who'd seen Jamie

70 · SUSAN RICHARDSON

as she was seeing him would fall for that one. He was as much man as she ever hoped to see—unself-conscious in his nakedness, proud and confident.

"You like fires, don't you?" she asked softly.

"I don't feel at home without one," he replied, not turning from his task. "It's an important source of heat at home, and most nights we need it."

She stared at him, curious. She wouldn't have thought Scotland was that primitive.

The fire was burning to Jamie's satisfaction now, so he turned his attention to Sarah. "Besides," he said with a slow smile that melted her insides, "you look incredibly beautiful by firelight."

"I was thinking the same thing about you."

"Beautiful?" he repeated indignantly. "I should hope not. Leave me some dignity, won't you?"

She smiled. He was joking, of course. Dignity was not something he would ever have to worry about. He had it in full measure. Would always have it, no matter how much he poked fun at himself. It was evident in his proud bearing, the almost arrogant tilt of his head.

She studied him as he rose and walked back to the bed. Yes, he was beautiful. His hair was nearly dry again, and his skin glowed.

"Are you cold?" he asked, feeling her still damp hair and the sheets. The sheets were soaked in spots from their dripping hair and bodies.

"A bit," she said, "but the fire will warm us."

"Do you have a hair dryer?" he asked. "The electric blower kind?"

"Yes," she answered in surprise. "Why?"

"Where is it?"

She gestured toward a drawer in her dresser, and

watched him curiously as he retrieved the dryer and plugged it in. Returning to the bed, he pointed the nozzle at the largest wet spot and turned the dryer on.

Sarah's gurgle of a laugh bubbled out. "You're crazy, do you know that?"

"Of course I do," he replied, unperturbed. "I'm not stupid."

When the spot was warm and dry, he sat down behind Sarah and turned the machine on her head. "I want your hair in a cloud again, so I can float to sleep on it," he said, his voice itself a caress.

Soon the soothing feeling of the warm air on her head and his hands lovingly sifting through her hair lulled Sarah into a lazy somnolence.

It was in this state of mind that she murmured, "My mother used to say that you had to be a little crazy to truly live. I think my father was fairly loony, in a very good way, of course."

Jamie chuckled. "Is she a nice lady, your mother?"

"The very nicest of ladies," Sarah said dreamily. "You remind me a little of her."

That surprised a crack of laughter from him. "It's my granny you bring to mind. She's tied for the nicest-of-ladies position with your mother."

They were quiet for a few minutes, each savoring the feeling of being so very well liked by the other.

It was astonishing, really, Sarah thought. They hardly knew each other, yet she felt as if they'd been best friends all their lives. The lovers part was new and unbelievably exciting, but the familiarity and comfort she felt with Jamie seemed to have been a part of her always. He really did remind her of her mother, and her father. It was that zany streak, the

72 · SUSAN RICHARDSON

uninhibited unconventionality of him, together with the warmth and humor. Jamie had the spark that added that something special to life. He rang all the bells inside her.

She was so wrapped in a sense of wonder that it took a moment for his words to register.

"Where is she now?" he asked.

"What?"

"Your mother. Where does she live?"

He felt Sarah actually flinch. In a voice different from any he'd yet heard her use, she said, "In heaven, they tell me." The words were flip and brittle, to hide, he guessed, pain that perhaps would never heal.

"Mine too," he said gently, and switched off the hair dryer. In the silence that followed its roar his quiet voice rang clearly. "Perhaps our mothers are friends up there. Possibly it was them decided to throw us together."

Sarah laughed, the tension leaving her as suddenly as it had come.

"That's something else we have in common, then," she said, reaching a comforting hand up to his cheek.

He turned his face into her palm to kiss it. "That and our fantastic fiddle playing?" he teased her.

He held her hand away from his face as it turned into a menacing claw. "Temper, temper," he chided her. "I never would have thought you'd be so sensitive on the subject of your instrumental expertise."

"Or lack thereof," she said. As he grinned, she sniffed and added, "We artists are all temperamental."

"I'll let you read the pitiful scribbles I turn out when I try to write, sometime," he said magnanimously. "Then you can enjoy a good gloat. My cousin says his six-year-old brother can do better."

"Do you come from a large family?" she asked somewhat wistfully.

"You could say that. There are round about a hundred and twenty of us."

"You're joking!"

"Honestly, I'm not. I come from an island, you see. Eilean Mhaol, in the Scottish Hebrides. Families there tend to intermarry. I truly am related to most of the people on the island to one degree or another. And I feel responsible for every one of them."

His voice was enigmatic, as it had been when he'd spoken of being a "happy-go-lucky fellow."

"Yes," he said, "I come from a very close family. Almost incestuous, you might say."

She stared at him, trying to fathom the undercurrents in his voice. There was pleasure and pride when he spoke of his family, she was sure of that, but it wasn't undiluted. Some ambiguity colored his attitudes.

"Do you have much family yourself?" he asked, feeling he'd said enough about his concerns. He watched with fascination as her eyes changed color, from bright silvery gray to a smoky opaque color. A shadowy look, with secrets in it.

But when she spoke her voice was light and casual. "Nothing like yours," she said. "I was raised by foster parents." She paused. "I'll get us some wine, if you would like some."

She'd skirted that topic neatly, he thought as he watched her wrap a silk kimono around her slim self and flit out of the room. She eluded him at other points too, he realized. As close as they had come,

74 • SUSAN RICHARDSON

he sensed there were whole areas of the map marked off as forbidden territory. She talked fairly freely about her mother, but she shied away from anything else about her past.

He'd find her out, though, wee Sarah Hughes, he promised himself. He noted without surprise that he wanted to know her pain as well as her joy. That was a switch for him. He went for the pleasure, as a rule.

When Sarah came back, wineglasses and bottle in hand, he reached out and took them from her. He set them on the floor beside the bed, then untied the belt of her kimono. "We didn't really want any wine," he said gently.

"We didn't?" she asked in surprise.

"No," he said, very sure, "we didn't."

"Why did we go get it, then?" she murmured, only half-listening for the answer as Jamie pushed the kimono off her shoulders and pulled her down beside him.

"We were trying to fob off that nosy Jamie McLeod," he said against her lips, his clever hands running the length of her.

"Oh." No, she thought, this would not be an easy man to control. Or resist.

"But we know that's a useless enterprise," he murmured into her ear, then lightly nipped it.

"We do? How do we know that?" Her skin tingled wherever he touched her.

"Well, we realize, of course, that said Jamie McLeod has the well-known second sight." This sentence was punctuated by teasing kisses across her lips and down her throat.

"Ah," she replied breathlessly, her hands lifting of

FIDDLIN' FOOL • 75

their own volition to smooth across the satin steel of his shoulders.

"Yes. It's a fairly common thing in the Hebrides, and I myself have developed it to a very fine pitch." He lifted himself up on one elbow so that he could look and touch his fill.

"I see," she whispered, gazing up at him.

"I hope you do." His tone was light, but she sensed a seriousness in his words. "There's no place to hide. Soon I'll know everything there is to know about you."

As if to prove his point, he found with his lips the secret pulse point in her neck. She arched with arousal at his erotic touch, all thought of concealment abandoned.

He buried his hands in her hair, as much for the feel of it as to hold her head where he wanted it while he plundered her mouth. There would be no evading for her this time, he vowed. No controlling, no backing off. He wanted to impress himself on her senses for all time.

It had begun too swiftly for Sarah to erect any defenses. His mouth demanded, his kiss long and deep. His tongue drove her so that she was moaning.

"Love me, Jamie," she pleaded when he lifted his head.

"I intend to, my bonny wee Sarah," he murmured, his voice threaded with husky laughter. "I fully intend to."

This was no gentle seduction. This was powerful demand, and Sarah was helpless to resist. She was carried beyond thought almost immediately as Jamie's mouth and hands explored every part of her body, every aspect of her responses.

76 • SUSAN RICHARDSON

He drew her breasts into his mouth and fed on the nipples till shudders shook her body. His hands glided over and into her, teasing but never stopping long enough to satisfy.

She was gasping and pleading, her own hands and body moving restlessly against him, creating a friction that neither of them would be able to hold out against for long.

"Please. Now," she begged him.

He took her wrists and held her hands above her head to keep her from driving him where he wasn't ready to go. He looked fiercely into her eyes with that determined look she'd seen before. His breathing was deep and loud; hers was short gasps. She stared back at him, mesmerized. Strangely, she was less afraid of this predatory side of him than she had been of the gently ruthless seducer. In his intent gaze and heavy breathing she read her own power.

She closed her eyes and let her head fall back. Her wrists went slack in his grip, and she lay open, silently offering herself to him.

"Dear heaven!" he muttered, himself capitulating with her surrender. He entered her slowly, infinitely careful, feeling all through his body the shudders that began for her with his first stroke.

"Look at me," he demanded. "I want you with me for this."

She opened her eyes and slowly focused on his face. He was right. It was another kind of hiding, this submerging in passion. But, oh, it was frightening to face him when so exposed! She didn't dare think of what he might see, but then, she hadn't considered what she might see.

FIDDLIN' FOOL • 77

As he began to move within her, his expression changed. The fierceness was gone, though the concentration remained. His eyes were a bright blue in the firelight and filled with warmth for her. She began to smile, while her heart pounded and her flesh melted. He was making love to her, Sarah Hughes, not just an attractive woman he'd met. He was seeing her and loving her.

"Jamie!" she cried, as the universe exploded into the sound of his name.

Seven

Sarah lay with her head against Jamie's warm, hard shoulder. She sighed and snuggled closer to him under the covers, loving the rise and fall of his chest with his breathing. Happiness filled her.

Their loving had been different the second time. Would it be different every time? she wondered. Jamie had not been gentle, at least not in the beginning. His mouth and hands had seared and branded. It had clearly been his intention to dominate, and she had been willing to have it that way this time. She wanted him to take her the way he wanted; she needed to feel his desire for her. And she trusted him.

Jamie's thoughts were not so clear. His black jealousy had dissipated, true. But his possessiveness was, if anything, stronger than ever. How could he have thought that first night that this would be just a fine little affair? And now what? he asked himself.

Under her ear his voice was such a pleasing low

78

rumble, it was a few moments before Sarah took in the meaning of his words.

"I think I've gone and fallen in love with you," he said with disgust. "Now what the hell am I going to do about that?"

Shock froze her blood. *What* had he said?

He felt the sudden rigidity of her body. Raising his head, he looked at her. She had her head tucked down so that all he could see was the top of it.

He rolled to one side to see her face, but she kept her chin tucked against her chest.

"Sarah," he said, cupping her chin in his hand, "look at me."

She reluctantly allowed him to raise her face. He swore under his breath at what he saw there. "Damn, Sarah, you don't understand."

In the moonlight filtering through the shades, her wide eyes were so deep a gray they seemed black. She was looking directly at him, but he knew she was closed to him. Her face was pale and carefully expressionless.

"I have no business falling in love with anyone," he said urgently, wanting her to understand, to come back, "much less with someone like you."

"You don't have to explain anything to me, Jamie," she said, marveling that her voice was calm and level. She felt as if she'd been kicked in the stomach. "I didn't make love to you with any conditions in mind."

He exhaled impatiently. "I know full well you didn't. But neither of us knew it would be what it is."

She had known, she thought. She had known from the start.

Aloud, she said, "You don't have to care for me, Jamie. But if you do, why should you mind?" In

80 · SUSAN RICHARDSON

spite of all her efforts to control her voice, it broke
slightly at the last.

His arm tightened around her. "I don't mind caring," he said. "I mind knowing that I can't do much
about it. The way I live means I don't have a lot to
offer a woman." He was silent for a moment, grop-
ing for the words to make her understand.

She stared at him fixedly. She was like a wounded
fawn, he thought, watching a hunter to see if he
would shoot or not.

Sarah was torn between wanting to know about
his life and wanting to hide in a closet, her hands
over her ears to protect herself from the pain of his
words. The desire to know was stronger.

"I don't want . . ." she began, then stopped. No,
that wasn't true. It was important to be honest.
"You don't have to offer me anything," she amended.
"But I would like to know about your life."

Reading pain and courageous determination in
her face, Jamie had to fight the urge to say the
words, any words, that would make everything all
right. But he couldn't. He, too, felt that what was
between them was too important for anything but
total truth.

"I'm on the road two thirds of the year," he said at
last, "never staying much longer than a week in any
one place. And the stationary days and weeks aren't
spent in luxurious lodgings with regular meals and
reasonable hours. It's not a normal life. No one except a musician could stand it.

"And I can't give it up. Even aside from the fact
that music is my life, I have an obligation to my
family. You remember, my family of a hundred and
twenty? The music brings in the tourist trade. I'm

FIDDLIN' FOOL · 81

an ambassador of a vanishing way of life and a struggling culture."

He paused, frowning and staring into space. When he spoke again, it was slowly. He chose his words with care.

"Then there's the third of my life I do spend in one place. Eilean Mhaol. It isn't very big and isn't very rich. In fact, it's very poor. Life is hard there, though it has its compensations." His face softened as he thought about some of the compensations. Clean air, open spaces, freedom, neighborliness.

"There are round about two hundred people on the island," he went on. "And most of them love it there, as I do." He said the last somewhat defiantly, looking at Sarah as if he thought she'd challenge his statement.

She looked steadily back, absorbing his words without reaction.

"We're a close-knit group." His mouth twisted wryly. "Which has its disadvantages," he added ironically, "but I know I'll never leave the island altogether. It's my home. It's where Granny is. And friends. And cousins."

Sarah nodded. She understood about clinging to one's home. One needed to have a firm grounding in this world. She'd leave her own home with great reluctance. And a home with a hundred plus relatives must be fairly close to heaven.

Jamie took a deep breath and released it slowly. "But it's no place for someone who hasn't been bred to it, the island. There are very few shops, and the only entertainments are the ones you make yourselves. Modern conveniences are few and far between."

Sarah wanted to cry, "I don't need those things. Do you think I grew up in a house like this one?"

82 · SUSAN RICHARDSON

But pride kept her silent, and Jamie's next words killed all desire in her to plead for a place in his life.

"And the incomer who earns a place in island life is a rare person indeed. It's not just a close-knit society; it's a well-nigh closed one."

Some little spark of hope sputtered and went out in Sarah's mind. He wouldn't want her with him. She wouldn't fit in.

A coldness spread through her body. She felt far away suddenly, as if she were looking at Jamie through a long tunnel lined with the people that hadn't wanted her, or weren't sure they wanted her, or wanted only certain aspects of her.

You fool, she told herself bitterly. Surely you should know better by now than to leave yourself open to this. Humiliation burned in her, along with a grief she stubbornly refused to acknowledge.

Both of them were silent, looking at the sheets and the walls while they thought their own thoughts.

At length pride stirred in Sarah. Pride had carried her through the black years. Pride would carry her now. Jamie would not think she was a pitiful, clinging creature who needed patting and comforting. He would never know the sense of loss she had experienced during his explanation.

She took a deep breath. "I see," she said, pasting a cheerful smile on her face. "And I couldn't leave my own home, either. So there's not a lot of meeting ground between us."

He looked at her bleakly. It was what he was saying, he thought. Why did it sound so much worse when she agreed with him?

She continued bravely. "But we can enjoy the times we do get to see each other, can't we?" To tell him she never wanted to see him again would be to admit how much she'd wanted a place in his life. Besides, she didn't believe she could deny herself what she could have of Jamie. She didn't have that much pride.

He exhaled harshly. His face was grim in the cold light, his brows drawn together in a frown. He didn't seem to be getting much comfort out of her making it easy for him, she thought.

He grabbed the bed covers at her throat and pulled them down with one broad sweep of his arm. Her head fell back as she pulled in a deep breath and held it. His gaze roamed the velvety shadows and milk-white slopes of her body.

"Aye, this we can enjoy," he said fiercely as he bent to place his mouth on her breast.

Breakfast the next morning was interesting. Again the hostility from Michael. Again Jamie entertaining both him and Tom in spite of themselves.

Sarah felt wonderful—and terrible. Jamie was staying, he'd told her, all that day, Friday, and leaving early Saturday morning for a concert in L.A. and some film negotiations. She wasn't sure what the story was on this film, if he was doing the score for it or what, but she was still too uncertain in their relationship to ask for too many details about his life. At least she didn't have to face his leaving for a while yet, so she decided just to take what joy she could from his being there.

So far she was managing well. Last night helped. It was hard to be despondent after a night of loving like Jamie provided. Her body fairly sang with well-being.

By that afternoon Sarah was having more diffi-

84 • SUSAN RICHARDSON

culty keeping the anguish at bay. It seemed to be tied inextricably to the pleasure. The more her joy in Jamie grew, the more the pain grew. And the joy grew moment by moment.

He'd gone to school with her, and it had been a day she'd never forget. He'd played his fiddle and led the children in little freeform dances. He'd wrestled with the boys and helped the boys and girls alike hammer and saw small things out of wood.

By the end of the morning he had a troop of small boys following him everywhere, imitating his walk and gazing at him in adoration.

"Sure you wouldn't like a job?" Sarah had teased him.

"Hmm." He'd pretended to ponder the offer. "I'll think about it. How much are you paying?"

"Not a lot, but the fringe benefits are excellent."

He'd grinned widely, his gaze scanning her tempting shape in faded jeans. "I'm sure they are. Perhaps we can discuss them further this evening. Or even this afternoon."

"Possibly," she'd said, head tilted to one side as her lips curved in a mischievous smile. "Possibly."

"Careful, girl," he'd growled softly. "Look at me like that and the children will have sex education on the curriculum before it's scheduled."

They hadn't been able to wait until evening to continue the discussion. The afternoon had been spent among tangled sheets in Sarah's darkened bedroom. Slivers of light shifting through the blinds striped their bodies as they twisted and turned in the age-old dance. Hands smoothed and tormented, breaths mingled in sighs and groans as together they rode and crested one powerful breaker after another.

FIDDLIN' FOOL • 85

Sarah, with a glowing sense of her own power, worshipped Jamie's body with lips, tongue, and fingertips. At least she'd have this, if nothing else, she told herself. His virility and male beauty were all hers to command. She stretched his endurance to its limits, reveling in the sights, textures, smells, and sounds of his body.

Finally they lay sprawled in exhaustion, like rag dolls carelessly dropped by a child.

Jamie stared down at Sarah as she lay with her eyes closed, her face a study in peace and beauty.

"It's almost more than human, your womanliness," he said in wonder, his voice low. "You are more woman than I ever dreamed existed."

She opened her eyes. Her giggle broke the spell and brought an answering grin from him. In sepulchral tones, she asked, "Haven't you heard of the succubus on Eilean Mhaol?"

He pinched her flank. "You're also a little devil," he said, bending to nip her flat stomach. As she squeaked, he pulled himself up to hover over her, his lips inches from hers.

"Do you think you're ready to go again?" he asked tenderly. His Nordic blue eyes were soft.

Her smile expressed her wonder and love. She nodded and slowly lifted heavy arms to wind them around his neck.

They stayed home that evening, as Tom and Michael were going out and neither of them wanted anything more than uninterrupted time together. They made a fire together, they cooked a meal together, and they loaded the dishwasher together.

Their lovemaking that night had a desperation

about it. Sarah's eyes were huge and dark as her gaze roamed and fastened on every part of Jamie, eager not to miss anything. His hands, usually so sensitive and gentle, tended to clutch and squeeze. Both of them had bruises and scratches where greed had driven the other too hard.

As the pale watery light of dawn began to filter through the blinds, they lay in each other's arms, their faces close. Neither of them had slept. Sarah had refused to throw away a second of this night. Their expressions were grave.

"I don't know when I'll get back," Jamie said.

Sarah squeezed her eyes shut in pain. When she opened them, they shone with tears. "I don't think I want to see you anymore, Jamie," she said in a small, tight voice.

He drew in a harsh breath and reared up over her. "Well, think again!" he said fiercely between clenched teeth. "What kind of nonsense is this?"

She turned her head to the side. The tears spilled over and a sob broke out. "I don't want to go through this another time," she said, gasping. "It's much worse than I thought it would be."

He looked down at her in fury and despair. Her eyes were tightly shut, but tears oozed out from between the lids, running in rivulets down her cheeks and onto the sheets. Her teeth gripped her bottom lip so that only small animal sounds escaped from her. But her body was shaking and shuddering with emotion.

With a groan ripped from deep inside him, he gathered her close. "Sarah, Sarah," he whispered. "How I love you. How I love you."

She cried harder at that, racking sounds of pain

FIDDLIN' FOOL · 87

torn from her. He held her close, gently smoothing her hair away from her hot, wet face.

When her storm of grief had quieted to small, hiccoughing gasps, he said softly, "The only thing harder would be not seeing each other, Sarah. I couldn't do it."

She lay still against his bare chest, damp from her tears. "I don't know," she said at last, her voice drained of emotion.

He rolled over to lie half across her. Putting one hand on either side of her head, he stared down at her. In the dim light his eyes gleamed, orbs of brightness. His gaze moved over her face as his thumbs caressed her cheeks and brows. He lowered his mouth to hers. She felt as if he were drawing her soul out through her lips, so fully did everything in her rise to meet him. "Jamie," she whispered.

"Say you love me," he demanded against her lips.

"I love you."

Her body arched in excruciating pleasure as he slid slowly and completely into her. He watched her eyelids quiver over her closed eyes.

Moving with agonizing care, he woke every nerve in her body to clamoring awareness. As he stroked her, he murmured into her ear, "You'll see me."

Borne along helplessly on the tide of sensation, Sarah knew that she would.

Jamie packed in silence as Sarah sat on the bed, miserably watching him. He shoved items viciously into his duffel bag, restrained impatience in every gesture. When everything was in, he zipped it up and stared at it.

Suddenly, he looked up at Sarah, hope lighting

88 • SUSAN RICHARDSON

his eyes. "Why don't you come to L.A. with me? It's a weekend, you don't have to work. Yes, that's it. Come with me." He leaned toward her, eagerness in every line of his body.

She slowly shook her head. "You'll be in meetings and rehearsals all day, Jamie. I'd only be in the way." He was going to argue. She could see it in his face. To forestall him, she added, "Besides, I have things I really should see to here. Gardening. A lunch date. And my story. The publisher wants to see it next month. I can't come. Really."

His expression became grim again. She watched him warily. She'd piled on the excuses. Would he buy them? He could so easily talk her into this, but she couldn't go with him. She didn't dare. Her roots had been too hard to come by for her just to rip them up to follow Jamie from concert to concert. She had to carry on with her daily life. She was going to need the haven of her routines in the coming weeks.

She'd chosen her excuses well. Jamie was thinking, Ach, no, of course not. Why should she disrupt her orderly life for a man who couldn't promise her anything but more partings? Damn these film negotiations! The tour schedule was manageable. He could get back between engagements. It was the interminable discussions of film rights, accommodations for the crew on Eilean Mhaol. There were times when he wished he'd never written his bloody book about Eilean Mhaol, never mind the revenue for the island.

"Right," he said in a clipped tone, swinging his duffel bag to his back and reaching for his fiddle. "Well, then, take care of yourself."

"Jamie," she said hesitantly.

"What?" he asked, almost belligerent.

"Please don't be angry with me. I'm doing what I can."

His eyes softened fractionally. "I'm not angry with you, Sarah," he said. Then his sense of humor surfaced and his mouth twisted into a wry smile. "Just at the bloody world."

He leaned down and kissed her once, hard and quickly. "Be seeing you," he promised. "Don't come out with me."

With three long strides he was gone.

Eight

Sarah felt like a yo-yo—up when she heard from Jamie, down in the between times. He called regularly. He sent postcards and letters. Once there were flowers. Not your typical long-stemmed roses or orchids, but a bouquet of heather and Scotch thistles that had her grinning all day. Now, how had he come up with that? she asked herself, shaking her head in disbelief. Only Jamie could have charmed that kind of an offering out of your basic self-respecting florist.

Another time it was a hat. A straw hat, with a leather band studded with metal spikes and sporting orange and purple feathers in the band. Sort of an L.A. punk rocker's gear for a day in the country, she decided. She and Michael laughed themselves silly over that one.

Michael was fairly mild on the subject of Jamie these days, partly because Sarah's low periods alternated with moments of dizzy happiness when Jamie

FIDDLIN' FOOL • 91

called or the mail brought his letters. Even Michael had to give Jamie credit for trying.

But Sarah was looking terrible. She'd lost weight in these two weeks that she couldn't afford. The lovely bones of her face looked as though they might come through her translucent skin at any time. And though she still smiled, there was a strain about her that made Michael and Tom anxious.

She laughed at them. "You two are like broody hens," she would tease. "You're going to make wonderful fathers. I'm fine. Truly. You're supposed to be sick when you're in love. Haven't you heard? It's part of it. You want me to do it right, don't you?"

Privately she was ashamed of herself. So where is your vaunted independence? she asked herself scornfully. You were never going to let a man reduce you to this, isn't that right? Get on with your life, you cream puff!

She lectured and scolded herself ceaselessly, then alternately patted herself on the back. At least she wasn't chasing him around the country the way she'd like to, she commended herself. At least she wasn't *doing* anything insane. She was only *feeling* crazy.

She knew how easy it would be for her just to forget everything—friends, work, the children—and follow Jamie from concert to concert, like the most dedicated groupie. She would not, she vowed fiercely to herself, jeopardize her carefully constructed stable life for what had to be a fleeting madness. She would not. She knew too well what it felt like to be rootless and homeless.

When Jamie finally did make it back for a flying two-hour visit, he was appalled at the way she looked.

"What have you been doing to yourself?" he de-

92 • SUSAN RICHARDSON

manded after he'd whirled her around and around the waiting room of the San Francisco airport by way of hello. She was laughing, her eyes were shining, and she really didn't look that bad. But he could feel the bones in her back, and the circles under her eyes didn't disappear just because she was happy.

"Thanks very much," she replied in assumed indignation. "It's good to see you too." Her misty smile took the sting out of her words. As the fact registered that he didn't look much better than she did, her smile faded. Her hands moved from around his neck to caress his face.

"You look tired," she said in concern. "Is the schedule that hectic?"

He grinned wickedly. "No, the schedule is manageable. Just. The exhaustion is your fault, actually."

She raised her brows in disbelief.

"Truly it is. It's the insomnia, don't you see? I lie awake thinking about you, then leap up screaming in frustration to pace the room before hurling myself into a cold shower and going back to bed to start the whole thing over again. In the Hebrides they'd call you a witch."

She smiled, appreciating as always his gift for exaggeration.

"That makes you a warlock then," she said. "Or is it a wizard?"

They both smiled, gazing at each other in pleasure for a long moment.

Jamie was the first to speak. "There's so much to say and not enough time. I don't know where to begin. Will we just make love here and count the public indecency charge well worth it?"

"Of course. Why not?" She picked up his fiddle

America's most popular, most compelling romance novels...

Here, at last...love stories that really involve you! Fresh, finely crafted novels with story lines so believable you'll feel you're actually living them! Characters you can relate to...exciting places to visit...unexpected plot twists...all in all, exciting romances that satisfy your mind and delight your heart.

EXAMINE 4 LOVESWEPT NOVELS FOR

15 Days FREE!

To introduce you to this fabulous service, you'll get four brand-new Loveswept releases not yet in the bookstores. These four exciting new titles are yours to examine for 15 days without obligation to buy. Keep them if you wish for just $9.95 plus postage and handling and any applicable sales tax.

☐ **YES,** please send me four new romances for a 15-day FREE examination. If I keep them, I will pay just $9.95 plus postage and handling and any applicable sales tax and you will enter my name on your preferred customer list to receive all four new Loveswept novels published each month *before* they are released to the bookstores—always on the same 15-day free examination basis.

20123

Name_____

Address_____

City_____

State_____ Zip_____

My Guarantee: I am never required to buy any shipment unless I wish. I may preview each shipment for 15 days. If I don't want it, I simply return the shipment within 15 days and owe nothing for it.

R 1234

Now you can be sure you'll never, ever miss a single Loveswept title by enrolling in our special reader's home delivery service. A service that will bring all four new Loveswept romances published every month into your home—and deliver them to you before they appear in the bookstores!

Examine 4 Loveswept Novels for

15 days FREE!

(SEE OTHER SIDE FOR DETAILS)

BUSINESS REPLY MAIL
FIRST-CLASS MAIL PERMIT NO. 2456 HICKSVILLE, NY

Postage will be paid by addressee

Loveswept

Bantam Books
P.O. Box 985
Hicksville, NY 11802

NO POSTAGE
NECESSARY
IF MAILED
IN THE
UNITED STATES

and linked her arm through his. "Are you hungry?" she continued on a more mundane level. "We could get a meal at the rather rotten restaurant here."

"Let's just talk," he said. "It's enough rather rotten meals I've had this week already." He led the way to a deserted row of padded seats. "So tell me all your doings. Has Michael been miscalling me right and left?"

"No, no, he's decided you're a very nice guy. He just thinks I'm a fool for agreeing with him."

"It's true," Jamie said adamantly. "I am a very nice guy. Are you sure you won't get onto this plane with me? We could have a grand time in Seattle."

She had to pretend he was joking, otherwise she'd have been heading for the ticket counter. "Could you count me as carry-on luggage?" she teased.

"Why not, if I carry you on?" His blue eyes bored into her gray ones as he recognized as always her evasive tactics.

"I want you with me, Sarah," he said seriously. "For the record, I want you with me anytime we can manage it. I'm not noble enough to just get out of your life. But I'll not pressure you, because I know I haven't a lot to offer. It's probably better off you are at home."

Sarah felt a pang in her midsection. What was this? she asked herself. Did she really want him to insist so that she could do what she was longing to without taking responsibility for it? Shame on you, Sarah Hughes.

This internal lecturing was getting to be a regular feature of life for her, she thought. It took constant vigilance to keep herself under control.

The parting was worse and better this time. Worse because she felt she'd hardly seen him. Better be-

94 · SUSAN RICHARDSON

cause he would be back in a week, this time to stay overnight.

And so it went. Jamie came and left twice more. Each time he asked Sarah to travel with him, and each time she refused. In Seattle he told himself he'd not come again. It was too hard on the both of them. But of course he did come back. And she was on his mind constantly. He was writing music at a terrific pace, and every song was for or about Sarah.

Soon he'd have enough for an entire album, he told himself ironically. Or ten. Wonderful. He'd spend his life thinking and singing about a woman he couldn't see more than once a month. And that was in the years he toured the U.S. What about those when he didn't?

He went round and round, trying to find a solution. His longtime friend Ian Grant, who was doing backup guitar with him for a concert in San Diego, told him repeatedly he was a fool.

"Yer makin' up problems, man," he told Jamie bluntly, uncharacteristically serious. "If she cares enough about you to put up with you disruptin' her life every week or so, she cares enough to want to be with you. I'd stake m'life on it, and I'm not often wrong about women. You know that fine."

"Why isn't she with me, then?" Jamie asked. "It's often enough I've asked her. If she can't bear the traveling life even for a weekend, what hope is there for a lifetime?"

"She's protectin' herself, ya bluidy fool! She thinks yer leavin' and she wants to have somethin' left when the time comes."

"And aren't I leaving?" Jamie snarled. "Next month

it's Kentucky and the festival, then home for the filming. What then?"

Ian smiled, unmoved by Jamie's bad temper. "Bein' in love's done nothin' fer yer disposition," he said. "Or fer yer wits. Take her with you. Joost take her with you. Yer makin' up problems, I'm tellin' you. She's got the summer off, hasn't she? And she can write as well in Kentucky or on the island as in her house, can't she? Take her with you. Give the both of you the summer to see if she'll take to the life."

Jamie glared at his friend ferociously, but he didn't seem to be seeing him. Ian smiled. He'd planted the seed. He'd wait now and see.

Jamie's tour was over. The arrangements to film his book on Eilean Mhaol later that summer had been finalized. In three days he flew to Kentucky to spend a couple of weeks preparing for and participating in the Celtic music festival. All that remained was to tell Sarah. He hadn't yet, fearing it would ruin these few days they had together.

But as he looked at her on the beach barefoot, and wearing a sweater and rolled-up jeans, he knew he wasn't leaving her. He'd take her with him if he had to stuff her into a trunk. Best tell her, he decided. She'd need time to make arrangements.

School was out for the year and Sarah had sent her new book off to her publisher. They had celebrated their mutual freedom by going for an overnight camping trip in Big Sur. It had been Jamie's idea. A sort of test, he'd admitted to himself, that Sarah had passed with flying colors. He had known she would, of course, or he'd not have done it. He was the one who needed the reassurance that she wasn't dependent on microwave ovens, electric blankets, and hot running water.

"Breakfast!" he called from his post beside the driftwood fire. He'd risen early to fish, happy to see that his Hebridean casting skills translated to the California coast.

Sarah looked up with a quick smile. She was wading, bent over in a search for sea life where the breakers spent themselves, hissing onto the shore.

"Mmm, smells wonderful," she said as she reached the fire and held out her finds for Jamie's inspection. "You're a man of many talents."

"What have you got there? Is it edible?" he asked, studying the tiny horseshoe crabs trying to burrow between Sarah's fingers.

"Certainly not. They're only babies!" she exclaimed. "I thought you'd like to admire them."

He smiled. "When you grow up on an island, nature's beauties tend to be viewed in terms of caloric value. Or weather prediction, if it happens to be a skyscape."

"Of course they would be," she said thoughtfully, reflecting, as she did every time she and Jamie were together, on how inevitably different their outlooks were. Perhaps that was one of the things she found so refreshing about him, she mused as she returned the tiny crabs to the sand.

They ate their fish and eggs in silence, except for Sarah's murmurs of appreciation. Jamie watched her, trying to decide how to tell her but constantly getting distracted by the way she looked and moved.

She'd washed her face in a splash of water from the water bottles they'd brought, and tied her hair up in a knot on the top of her head. She looked as fresh as the ocean, he thought, with the delicate color in her cheeks and her eyes shining and clear. She wore little makeup at any time, and her face was one that could carry it off, supplying its own color and shape. Her clothes tended to be chosen for comfort and durability as well as for style. She was a casual, natural woman, not needing beauty products to bolster her confidence.

It might just work, he told himself, excitement stirring within him. It might just work out between them.

He tossed his head back to drain the last of the coffee from his mug. Vile stuff. He'd never get used to it. Thank heavens he'd be within reach of a decent cup of tea before long.

Sarah smiled at his grimace of distaste. "Why do you drink it if you hate it?" she asked.

"For the caffeine. Purely for the caffeine. I'm a caffeine junkie."

"And I suppose you down vast quantities of that tannic acid brew the English like when you're at home."

"Too right I do. I'll have you swearing by the stuff, too, before we're through."

A funny look crossed Sarah's face. Mention of the future was rare between them. They'd studiously avoided the subject since their initial agreement that a future for them was unlikely.

"The film negotiations have been finalized," Jamie said casually, though he was watching her intently.

Her gaze flew to his. Any hint of finality in the present arrangement was cause for alarm. "Oh?" she asked brightly, trying to disguise her disquiet. "You know, I've never really been clear on what the film was about. I'd heard you were to star in one, of course. But what's the story?"

98 • SUSAN RICHARDSON

Jamie threw back his head and roared. Sarah stared in amazement as his shouts of laughter startled several nearby gulls into wheeling, raucous flight.

"*What* is so funny?" she asked when Jamie was weakly chuckling and wiping his eyes.

"Me, a movie star," he said, grinning. "Can you imagine it?" He shook his head in astonished delight.

Sarah was grinning too. It was impossible not to in the face of his mirth, but she was puzzled. "Then what were all the negotiations about?"

"About my book." He pronounced it to rhyme with "Luke." "They're going to film my book. And I wanted to make sure it was done on the island, so the islanders would get something out of it."

"You wrote a book?" she asked accusingly. "I thought you said you couldn't write!"

"I said my writing was pitiful, and so it is from the literary standpoint. But the subject matter is sensational enough for a film, never mind the writing style."

"I'm astonished! Why didn't you tell me? I could have read it!"

He assumed an expression of wounded pride. "Now you've hurt my feelings. I thought everyone had read it."

Sarah was beaming with pleasure. "You wrote a book! How marvelous. I can read it when you're away. It will be like having a conversation with you. What's it about?"

His expression softened to tenderness. She was blazing with eagerness, leaning toward him in her excitement.

"It's really a sort of travelogue," he explained, "with character sketches and scraps of conversation with islanders. But it has some of the more sensational

FIDDLIN' FOOL • 99

historical happenings in it, in anecdote form, and it's one of these they're filming. A tribal feud sort of story, with the McLeods of Eilean Mhaol outsmarting the McAskills of Brunha, of course. It's a rare old story, actually, what with hiding in the caves and clambering up the rock faces and sea battles and beautiful clanswomen leading their foes into the bogs. Good fun for everyone. Lots of seduction and gore."

"I can't wait to read it!" Sarah said. "Do you have copies with you?"

"An autographed copy awaits you at home," he promised grandly. He laughed when Sarah looked as if she might leap up and start for home that minute. "Here, look! You can have a real conversation with the author himself just now. So set yourself down."

She grinned somewhat sheepishly. She did tend to get carried away with her enthusiasm.

Jamie eyed her fondly. "Come over here, wee beauty," he said, patting the sand beside him as he leaned back against a piece of driftwood. "You're too far away."

She complied happily and was tucked warmly against Jamie's side. They were silent for a bit, watching the early morning clarity of the sky and listening to the crash and hiss of the waves as they advanced and receded.

"Tide's going out," Jamie said quietly.

"How do you know that?" Sarah asked.

He looked at her curiously. "Do you mean to say you don't?"

She shook her head. Here was another of those differences, she thought. On the beach it was very apparent. Jamie was completely at home with the natural world. He was the sort of person who could survive handily in the wilderness or on a deserted

100 • SUSAN RICHARDSON

island. She looked at his calm strong face against the backdrop of the sea and thought how it fit into that setting.

"I'm a city girl," she said. "You're so much more in tune with the world than I am. I wish you had time to teach me."

He smiled down at her happily. It was as if he were writing her lines this morning. "Perhaps we'll have the time," he said gently. Then, taking a slow breath, he continued. "Sarah, you know the festival is in about three weeks?"

"Yes?" Dread filled her chest like lead. They'd talked about the festival. She knew Jamie had been working on it for more than a year. Musicians from all over the globe would be congregating in the mountains of Kentucky to produce the festival—a series of concerts and workshops on every aspect of Celtic music. Jamie was hosting it, and a public broadcasting network would be concurrently filming a documentary on the making of the festival.

Sarah had even known the date, but she had refused to think about it, knowing that when it was time for the festival, Jamie would be gone. And after the festival, he'd be on Eilean Mhaol making a film.

She didn't want him to tell her about it. She knew she'd cry or do something equally embarrassing. She started to rise. She'd get more coffee, collect shells, do something.

But Jamie held her with a firm pressure on one arm. "Sarah," he said, his voice low and serious, "I have to go in three days time."

A little whimper of pain escaped before she could catch it. She turned her head toward the ocean, seeing nothing, hoping to gain time and control.

Jamie felt the rigidity in her body. He ached to

soothe her, but a canny director's voice in his head was saying, Not yet. Not yet. Let it sink in.

At the thought of leaving her, he felt his own jaw clench in pain. She would come with him. She had to come with him.

Sarah felt as if she were dying. Anguish tore and raged through her body. Jamie was leaving. Life without Jamie. Life without joy. She didn't think she could stand it. What could she do? Little helpless questions chased themselves around and around her numbed brain.

When the director in him felt she'd had enough time to consider the consequences of letting him go, Jamie stated his case.

"Come with me, Sarah," he said. It took all his will not to plead. "Come away with me. I can't leave you behind. It would tear the heart out of me." It wasn't begging, but the hoarseness of his voice hid nothing of his feelings.

As his words registered, Sarah felt relief pour through her veins like adrenaline. She drew a deep breath, turned, and hurled herself into Jamie's arms.

He embraced her and lay his head on top of hers, hope making him feel shaky. She hasn't refused. She hasn't said no.

Sarah drew back, her eyes huge and shining with mingled joy and apprehension as she looked at him.

"Do you mean that?" she asked intensely.

"Of course I mean it! Will you come?"

She studied his face, which looked as vulnerable now as she'd ever seen it, and took a deep breath. "I guess I'll have to," she said slowly in a tone of wonder. "Waving you off at the airport doesn't bear thinking of."

But she had to double check. "Jamie, are you

102 • SUSAN RICHARDSON

really sure? What about your friends—the other organizers? What are they going to think about having a strange female deposited on them?"

He couldn't resist. Relief made him feel silly. "You're not so strange," he said, straightfaced.

She made a little move. "And I guess they must be used to strangeness," she said, casting a meaningful look his way.

Suddenly giddiness overtook both of them. Jamie made a hideous face and lunged menacingly toward her. She rolled nimbly out of the way and leaped to her feet, pelting him with a fistful of sand as she dodged away from the fire.

"Oh-ho, so it's dirty you're fighting, is it?" he said. Leering, he limped after her, Quasimodo-style. She shrieked in pretended alarm and sprinted off down the beach.

Soon it was a chase in earnest, as Jamie put on speed and she zigzagged and swerved, using her agility to keep out of his reach for a few seconds until the inevitable conclusion of the contest.

She was laughing too hard to elude him for long, but as his hands closed over her arms at the water's edge, she hooked her foot around his ankle and tugged. They went down together, Sarah underneath Jamie. He took the brunt of his weight on his own arms, but even so, Sarah felt as if she'd been bombed.

"Oof!" she grunted.

"Are you all right?" he asked in concern. But then the wave that had been building behind them broke and rolled over them, making Sarah's squashing a secondary concern.

She shrieked and he bellowed as the icy water soaked them. Sarah in particular, being on the bot-

FIDDLIN' FOOL • 103

tom, was quickly wet through—hair, clothes, and skin.

In a belated chivalrous gesture, Jamie rolled so that Sarah was on top and he was lying in the receding pool of water.

She giggled helplessly as the cold water seeped through to his skin, making him yelp. "Damn!" he cursed. "What is it with you and water? Am I to be half-drowned every time I make love to you?"

Through her laughter she said, "You can't make love to me here."

The look on his face caught her and she repeated in alarm, "Jamie, you can't! It's a public place."

He rolled again so that Sarah was beneath him and his smiling but determined face hung inches away from hers.

"Never say *can't* to a Scottish male," he advised her. "It makes them crazy. Besides, your American public's far too lazy to be up at this hour."

She took a deep breath and gazed up at him, fascinated. Without taking his eyes from hers, he reached between them and unzipped and unsnapped first her jeans, then his. Her breath was coming fast, her chest rising and falling erratically.

His eyes gleamed, and he bared his teeth in a wicked smile as he raised himself above her and raked her body with his gaze. The wet, clinging clothes faithfully outlined every curve. "You make me crazy," he whispered, lowering his lips to hers.

Sarah was melting and freezing at the same time. She shivered, whether from cold or excitement she couldn't be sure. The pale stubble on Jamie's face scraped her cheeks and the skin around her lips. His tongue caressed her mouth as he entered her outrageously, audaciously.

104 • SUSAN RICHARDSON

"It's not our usual style, perhaps," he whispered, his voice laced with laughter as they rolled together in the waves.

Sarah wasn't complaining.

The next three days passed in a flurry of preparations. There were tickets to buy, clothes to pack. Jamie made the simplest shopping expedition a frolic.

"Boots, that's the thing," he insisted in one store. He shoved her into a chair and trotted out several pairs of hiking boots, a hundred dollars or more a pair. "We can buy raingear there, but you'd better have your climbing boots from here."

"Raingear?" Sarah asked weakly. "It's going to be summer soon. Why will I need raingear?"

"What a provincial little ignoramus it is," he replied scornfully. "I can see I'll have to take your education in hand. In places other than California and the Sahara, it rains in the summer months."

He talked her into trying on a dress he'd seen in a boutique window—a neoromantic creation made of old lace, creamy with age and delicate. It had a high throat-hugging neckline, long sleeves, and a graceful fall of lace for the skirt. The bodice was tight, showing off her high breasts and tiny waist. She pirouetted for him, and the look in his eyes made her feel shy.

He said nothing. He just stared, a small smile on his face. In that dress, he thought, she looked what he felt her to be—something rare and precious, fragile yet with strength enough to last for generations. Fey and not quite of this world, but as fluid and sensual as water and bird song. He nodded at the sales clerk and wrote a check for heaven-knows-what, ignoring Sarah's half-alarmed, half-delighted protests.

"It will do fine for the first night of the festival," he told her. "You'll want something special that night."

His expression as he said that was so strange, she stared at him. "Is that a prophesy?" she asked uneasily.

He smiled enigmatically. "Aye, that it is," he said, nodding. "That it is."

Finally they stood in a line at the airport, waiting to board their plane. Michael and Tom were alongside them.

Sarah turned to Tom for a good-bye hug. "Take care of yourself," she said.

"I will," he promised. "And you write us as soon as you get there. We'll be waiting to hear that you're settled in."

Michael stuck out a hand for Jamie to shake. "Take care of her," he commanded. "Or we'll kill you." He accompanied his threat with a cheerful grin.

Jamie smiled back. "She'll have more people looking after her there than she does here," he said.

Sarah hugged Michael. "Don't let my houseplants die," she pleaded. "And the fruit trees need a final spraying."

"Yes, yes, stop worrying," he said. "It's only for a month. The place will look better when you get back than it does now."

A quick good-bye, some waves, and she and Jamie were through the door to the boarding ramp.

Jamie installed Sarah in the window seat, saying he'd had enough views from airplanes to last him a lifetime. She sat with her nose glued to the window.

106 • SUSAN RICHARDSON

This was her third flight, but she felt it was the most important move she'd ever made. She was excited, but nervous.

Jamie took one of her small, cold hands in his. She flashed him a quick smile before turning back to watch the runway roll by.

He looked at her broodingly. Michael's remark about finding the place in order when she returned had flicked him on a tender spot. Aye, that was it, he told himself. There had not been a thing so far to suggest she was considering coming on with him to Eilean Mhaol. All her arrangements proclaimed she was merely making a visit to Kentucky, not considering whether or not she wanted to share his life, as he'd meant her to do. *Give us a chance, lass,* he pleaded silently.

Sarah was still staring out the window. The plane was picking up speed. They were airborne. In minutes the big jet wheeled and headed east. She watched the airport shrink and imagined Tom and Michael, her house, the school, all the familiar aspects of her life receding behind her.

What had she done? she asked herself in panic. She shouldn't have come! What was she away from her place in the world?

Jamie felt her hand clench convulsively into a fist, and abruptly his perspective shifted. Why, the lass was frightened, he realized. She was as pale as a sheet.

It must be a wrench, he thought. She'd never had a place of her own till lately, and now was leaving it. With her background, the temptation to cling to a toehold must be strong. For him it was different. He knew where home was. He could come and go as often as he pleased, assured it would always be there for him to go back to. He was going home now, indirectly, but Sarah was going far out on a limb.

Warmth filled him. As he stroked her taut fist, he made her a silent promise. You won't regret it, lass, he vowed. He'd make sure she didn't regret it. They'd make some sort of life together, even if he had to give up his own home. Even if he had to sell insurance to buy the bread.

Slowly the fact that Jamie's warm fingers were stroking her cold ones penetrated Sarah's consciousness. Her hand closed on his, and she squeezed as tightly as she could, feeling the size and strength of his hand. Jamie. Jamie was her connection to the world. He was her present. And maybe even her future. Her courage began to return and she smiled at him.

"It will be all right, Sarah," he said.

"Possibly," she agreed, with dawning hope rising in her. "Just possibly."

Nine

Jamie's friend Ian Grant met them at the airport in Fort Knox, Tennessee. Sarah liked him on sight, with his friendly freckled face and exuberant manner.

"So this is Sarah," he said to Jamie, pumping her hand and beaming. "And now I'm seeing why you've been keeping her to yerself all this time. She's beautiful, Jamie. Can I give yer girl a welcome kiss?"

Sarah knew from the roguish gleam in Ian's bright blue eyes that he was teasing. She was sure outrageous comments to the ladies were standard for him, but Jamie was taking no chances.

"No," he replied succinctly, glaring at his closest friend. "Not ever. No to you of all people. Just keep a reasonable distance between you and Sarah. Say, ten feet."

"There's friendship for you," Ian said plaintively to Sarah. "And wasn't it me gettin' the young man his start in the musical worrrld?"

"And wasn't it my own cousin," Jamie shot back, "told me never to leave her alone with you, before we

108

FIDDLIN' FOOL • *109*

got her safely married off to yon doctor chap in Glasgow?"

Ian's eyes twinkled, but his expression was both innocent and aggrieved. "A suspicious woman, Margaret," he said righteously.

As he spoke he was shepherding them down a corridor to the baggage-claim area.

"You'll pay no attention to this jealous, mean-spirited fellow, Sarah," he went on. "You and I are going to be great friends."

Sarah laughed. She felt a little as if she had been run down by a steamroller, but somehow felt claimed and welcomed as well. She liked Ian Grant.

Sarah was sandwiched between the two men in the front seat of Ian's car. As they headed out of Fort Knox and into the rolling foothills of the Cumberland Mountains, Jamie asked Ian, "How are things shaping up at the site?"

"Well enough, well enough. It's a grand old place, the inn. A bit better than our usual accommodations. Working for the television people certainly upgrades the lifestyle. They do things right." He turned to look down at Sarah. "You'll like it, Sarah. We've got steep cliffs behind us and the river at our feet. Spectacular views. Plus a rather cracked but functional swimming pool and a couple of weedy tennis courts."

Jamie had given Sarah only the barest details about the place. "It's an operating resort hotel still?" she asked.

"Oh, aye," Ian replied, "though just barely, I believe. The place is crying out for repairs. That's why they've rented it to the television studios for the month. The profits will pay for repairs. Without the

110 • SUSAN RICHARDSON

repairs, I doubt they'd be able to go on much longer. It's a good thing for both sides. George and Venetta Luttrell, who own the place, are good people. I'm particularly fond of Venetta."

Jamie grinned. "Which means, if I know you, and I do, that she's a good cook and you've made her your slave already. Room service, no doubt. All your favorite dishes."

Sarah and Jamie laughed as Ian protested weakly. "Here, now, can I help my unfortunate affect on members of the opposite sex? It's the little-boy quality in me. Brings out the mother in women."

Jamie hooted and rolled his eyes. "Aye, any number of them have turned into mothers after a time in your company," he said ribaldly.

Sarah judged it time to change the subject. "Are there many people at the inn already who'll be working on the festival?"

"A few," Ian said. His face took on a disgusted look. "Gusher's there, of course."

Sarah laughed. "Gusher?" she repeated incredulously.

Jamie was amused. "Your old favorite!" he exclaimed, reaching behind Sarah to slap Ian on the shoulder.

Ian just snorted.

To Sarah, Jamie explained, "Gusher's probably the best of the Scottish whistle players. And a rather colorful character." He grinned broadly. "He and Ian hit it off so well that we simply couldn't do a show without him."

Ian snorted again, more profoundly. "Gusher couldn't wait to stick his oar in. He's constituted himself steward of the household. Handing out room assignments, if you can believe it."

FIDDLIN' FOOL • 111

"That's not his name," Sarah said with certainty.

" 'Gusher'?" Jamie asked. "Well, to begin with it was Guthrie. Guthrie Dowie. Gusher does rather fit, though, and he may find when this month with Ian is over that it's his to keep."

Ian's expression lost its grimness as he chuckled. "Gusher's a rather effusive type," he said, clearly understating the case. "Very unScottish. You'll see." He hesitated. "Patsy's there as well." He kept his gaze on the road, and his voice was so carefully expressionless that Sarah glanced at him curiously.

Jamie, too, stared out the window as he replied blandly, "You brought her along, did you?" There was a noticeable pause. "Well, that's good. Patsy always makes herself useful."

Sarah stared at Jamie in turn. Who was Patsy? There were unmistakable undercurrents here. The feeling of being an incurable outsider again swept over her, but that feeling was difficult to sustain around Ian.

" 'Useful,' " he repeated with a return of his warm smile. "You see, Sarah, why this hard-headed bloke is organizing the festival instead of a kindly soul like meself. He thinks of people in terms of their use. You'd best carve out a niche for yerself quickly here before yon power-mad fellow does it for you."

Still looking out the window, Jamie said thoughtfully, "If only they had put him on the pipes instead of the guitar, there'd have been a *use* for all that hot air." They all laughed at that one.

Sarah thoroughly enjoyed the trip to the inn sitting between the two bantering, good-natured men. The increasingly mountainous countryside was beautiful. The hills were thickly covered with laurel and rhododendron, and the ridges showed stands of yel-

112 · SUSAN RICHARDSON

low pine or a mixed growth of hemlock, magnolia, dogwood, holly, and oak. They drove through the Cumberland Gap and into Kentucky.

Jamie and Ian laughed as she exclaimed and rhapsodized over views of blue and purple mountains, or the light reflected off a lake tucked into a green valley. "We'll have to call you Gusher," Ian threatened, "and find another name for our whistling friend."

When they rounded a bend and caught their first sight of the inn, however, Sarah was too stunned to gush. The fading afternoon light gleamed on the limestone that formed the base of the building and competed with the sparkle of the river rushing below. Long, sloping lawns surrounded the rambling two-story wood-frame-and-stone structure. A two-story porch extended across the entire facade. Sarah fell instantly and deeply in love with it.

"Look at her face," Ian said, not entirely joking. "If someone looked at me the way she's looking at that building, I wouldn't be a bachelor."

"It's heavenly," Sarah murmured, unabashed.

Jamie glanced down at her, then smiled fondly as she continued to gaze in unapologetic rapture at the inn. She was enjoying this, he thought happily. She was loving seeing all these new things and places. Perhaps she'd take to traveling after all.

Aloud, he kept it light. "Ach, she thought she'd be billeted in a cave, I don't doubt."

Ian looked with wry exasperation at his friend. "Been telling her horror stories about the musician's life, have you?" They pulled to a stop in front of the inn before Jamie could retort. "I see our welcoming committee's on hand," Ian warned them.

Three people were on the porch—an older couple,

both thin and angular, with warm, shy smiles, and a short, rotund man with cheeks like shiny apples. His wholesome-looking face was oddly at variance with his ultrafashionable getup. He had a punk haircut, one dangly gold earring, and was wearing a black shirt, jeans, and boots.

This vision rushed down the steps, hands outstretched, as the three of them climbed from the car. "Jamie, welcome, thrice welcome! How lovely to see you! We've been awaiting your arrival breathlessly!"

The man was somewhat breathless. Jamie took his outstretched hands and smiled. "Hello, Guthrie." Actually, it came out more like "Gushrie." Sarah was sure that was accidental, though, because Jamie shot Ian a quelling look as another snort forced its way out.

Guthrie shot Jamie a swift, suspicious glare, but was reassured by Jamie's smile. It was a gift Jamie had, Sarah thought. That tolerance for seemingly the whole world. He truly liked people, all people, quirks, foibles, and all.

"Guthrie," he said, drawing her forward, "meet Sarah, a very special friend of mine. Sarah, this little ray of sunshine is Guthrie Dowie, a fearfully efficient organizer of picky details and a fierce player of the whistles."

"How do you do?" Sarah said, offering her hand.

Guthrie took it and bowed with a flourish. "Delighted," he said.

"Sarah will be staying the month, Guthrie."

The delight fled. Guthrie's eyebrows shot up ludicrously, and he looked anything but pleased at the news. "Oh," he said, looking back and forth at the two of them, "but we didn't plan . . . That is, I didn't

114 • SUSAN RICHARDSON

know . . . I mean, where are we to put her? In with you? Or . . ."

Jamie watched this remarkable performance with amusement, obviously feeling none of the awkwardness Sarah herself was experiencing. As he turned toward her, unholy glee on his face, she realized he wasn't about to bail her out of this situation.

"Where would you like to be *put*, Sarah?" he asked reasonably, mirth brimming in his eyes.

With a final disgusted snort, Ian exited the scene to greet the Luttrells at the top of the stairs.

Sarah sent Jamie a smile that promised revenge. "Oh, in a room of my own, if possible," she said in a terribly sweet voice. "So useful to have a place you can throw people out of."

Jamie chuckled admiringly.

Guthrie's ditherings were cut short as Ian brought the Luttrells down to be introduced. Sarah thought they were lovely people, with their slow, gracious Kentucky voices and gentle manners. Venetta Luttrell eased the awkwardness of the room assignments by asking Sarah which bags were hers. George gathered them up and followed as Venetta ushered Sarah into the house.

"I have a nice room with a river view that I think you'll enjoy, Sarah," she said softly. "Won't you come upstairs?"

As Sarah gratefully climbed the stairs with Venetta, she glanced back just as Ian asked, "Anyone else check in, Gusher?"

Guthrie puffed himself up and spat out, "Don't call me that, you . . . Jamie, did you hear what he called me? I'm not putting up with that sort of—"

Jamie put a hand on each of their shoulders smiling wryly. "Boys, boys," he said, "we'll arrange a

FIDDLIN' FOOL • 115

duel later. For the now, could you just agree to avoid each other? Perhaps the silent treatment would be effective?"

Sarah smiled to herself as the stairs cut off the sound and sight from below. Producing this festival was going to be no easy task for Jamie.

She was unpacking when a knock sounded on the door. Before she could speak, Ian's sandy-haired head popped in. "Hello, are you settling in?" he asked.

She smiled. "Yes. And you came out of the battle with a whole skin, I see."

A scornful expression on his face, he entered the room. "Battle! The best that runt could manage is name-calling." He grinned. "And he's not even very good at that. I'm a throwback, he says. To what, I don't know."

Sarah smiled again and went on with her unpacking. Ian sat on her bed and leaned back on his forearms, watching her with interest.

"So you're the famous Sarah," he said musingly.

She slanted him an ironic look. "You're just figuring that out?"

He ignored that. "At first I was pleased for Jamie," he said, "but now . . . Are you sure you wouldn't rather be with me?"

Sarah's lips twitched. It must be second nature for Ian to flirt with any woman he saw. She didn't bother with an answer.

"Does Jamie know you're here?" she asked curiously.

Ian grinned. "No. There really might be a battle then, eh?"

He continued to look at her thoughtfully. "You're not quite what I expected," he said finally. It was the fragile quality about her that had him worried. He'd encouraged Jamie to bring her here, but upon seeing

116 • SUSAN RICHARDSON

her, he was feeling an unexpected sense of responsibility. He hoped this was all going to turn out all right. "What ever are your friends thinkin' of to let you travel around with a strange man?" he demanded.

"He's not so strange," she said, one corner of her mouth lifting as she remembered Jamie saying the same thing about her.

"None stranger," Ian said, and suddenly they were grinning at each other in shared understanding and love for Jamie. "None stranger," Ian repeated with an emphatic nod of his head. Sarah didn't deny it.

"And," Ian continued, "honesty forces me to admit I'm a close second. But I would like you to know that Jamie's not the only strange fellow here who would go out of his way to help you. You're to tell me if you need anything and you don't want to ask Jamie. Understood?" He waited until she'd nodded, then heaved himself off the bed. He winked, said, "See you later," and left.

Warmth flooded Sarah. She'd found a friend. She'd come all this way feeling shaky and sure she'd be an outsider, and she'd immediately found a friend. Her spirits soared and she twirled around the room in elation. She was in love with a man who loved her, she was in one of the loveliest places she could have imagined, and she had a new friend. What could possibly go wrong?

The next knock on the door heralded Jamie. He gave her a quick kiss before critically testing the bed.

"Thinking you might like to trade rooms, are you?" she asked sarcastically, hands on hips.

He grinned. "No need for that," he said cheerfully.

She glared at him, trying not to laugh. Cocky devil. There wasn't a doubt in his mind but that he'd be sharing that bed.

FIDDLIN' FOOL • 117

He sauntered over to her and took her in his arms, completely unmoved by her glowering expression. "There are a number of people here already," he said, "and a few more arriving tonight. It looks like we're having a *ceilidh*." He used the Gaelic word for an impromptu gathering. "Do you mind?"

"Of course I don't mind," she said, and smiled guilelessly. "I'll entertain your friends on my fiddle."

"You'll sit in the corner quietly like a good little girl," Jamie commanded. "And for heaven's sake, wear something ugly. The only thing I mind about having all my friends on the premises is that I'll be busier than they will. Some of them might take it into their heads to keep you company."

"Well, I might need someone to console me when you're not around," she teased.

He scowled. "Careful. I wouldn't like to have to murder one of my friends."

His tone was just sincere enough to make Sarah relent. She linked her arms on his neck. "I'm only teasing," she whispered into his ear. "There's no room for anyone else in my mind at the present."

He drew her close and lowered his head to press his lips against her neck. He groaned. "Maybe it was a mistake bringing you along. How am I going to concentrate on my work when this is what I could be doing?"

From below they heard a faint shout. "Jamie! Has anyone seen Jamie?"

Jamie sighed, his breath warm against her skin. "I'd better go," he murmured. "They're all wanting a word with me." He raised his head and they smiled into each other's eyes. "Just wander around if you like," he suggested. "Explore the place. Introduce yourself to people. I'll see you later, before the *ceilidh*."

118 • SUSAN RICHARDSON

"All right," she said. "Bye." But the last was said to the air. Jamie was gone. She stared thoughtfully at the door for a moment. In their times together so far, she had been the one who'd had commitments and it was Jamie who had tagged along. Here it was going to be different. She had a feeling she'd better get used to seeing Jamie on the run.

She finished unpacking, then walked down the hall to see what—and who—she could find.

She found no one at first. She heard voices, even snatches of music, in the distance, but wasn't sure from where, and she didn't see a soul.

The inn was lovely, with its mellow paneled walls and huge stone fireplaces here and there. Sarah thought it had a faintly melancholy air, though, stripped as it was to the bare essentials of furnishings, and empty. It would be better later, perhaps, when it was full of people.

She wandered into the kitchen and almost missed the young woman sitting in the shadows. She was perched on a stool, peeling potatoes. Her hair was black, and she, like Guthrie, was dressed completely in black. A black oversize sweater that came below her hips, a straight, mid-calf black skirt, black tights, and low back boots with white socks. What was it with black these days? Sarah wondered.

With her own fluffy blonde hair and soft coloring, there could have been no greater contrast between her and the pale, dark-haired woman.

"Oh!" Sarah said when she realized she wasn't alone in the kitchen. "I didn't see you."

The woman turned heavily madeup eyes on her. "I'm Patsy," she said without preamble.

Sarah smiled tentatively. "Hello. I'm Sarah."

Patsy continued to stare at her curiously. She

wasn't unfriendly, but she didn't seem to feel any compulsion to smile, either.

"You're with Jamie," Patsy said.

"That's right."

"I'm with Ian. There will be several of us here. Donald's bringing Mary too."

Sarah stared at Patsy blankly. "Us?" she repeated.

Patsy stared back assessingly. "Yes, 'us.' Girlfriends. Camp followers, if you will." Her pale mouth formed a cynical little smile as she gauged Sarah's reaction to her remark.

Sarah stared at the wall just beyond Patsy's head. Her lips tightened as she mulled this one over. She'd always thought she was fairly modern in her out-look—she wasn't trying to hide the fact that she and Jamie were lovers—but she didn't care for being grouped with the other musicians' live-in companions.

She lifted her head proudly, defiantly, as she looked back at Patsy. Patsy was still watching her with that cynical assessment. Sarah knew she was being prim and snobbish, but she couldn't help herself. She wouldn't even be here if she hadn't convinced her-self she was more than just another girlfriend to Jamie. She wasn't a good enough actress to pretend a casualness she didn't feel.

Patsy's lips twitched with what could have been amusement—or the same self-mockery that showed in her words. "You mustn't mind me," she said. "I'm just being petty. I used to be with Jamie, you see."

Sarah sharply drew in a breath, then let it out slowly. "Oh," was all she could manage. A curious numbness spread outward from her stomach. She smiled stiffly, but inside she was shouting, What? Was she going to trip over Jamie's past in every room here? What kind of a life did he lead?

120 • SUSAN RICHARDSON

Beyond the shock and instinctive recoiling, jealousy was clawing at her. She wanted to scream something idiotic, like, Don't you dare even remember that! Don't even look at him again!

"Yes," Patsy continued. "He's good, isn't he?"

At the expression on Sarah's face, Patsy threw up her hands as if to ward off an attack and laughed, a surprisingly merry sound. "Don't shoot!" she said, amused. "I've finished being a bitch. It's all out of my system."

Sarah's eyes were still flashing, but her mouth was also quivering as she fought unexpected tears. Patsy took in both reactions, her head tilted to one side.

"Hey," she said finally, "you don't look tough enough to survive the likes of me. And the entertainment world's full of us. Are you all right?"

Sarah nodded stiffly. She pulled out a stool at her end of the counter and sank onto it, feeling she'd be stronger sitting down.

"Well," Patsy said, "I always think it's better to have things out in the open. But I guess it must have been a shock. Jamie didn't tell you about me?"

"No," Sarah said quietly.

Patsy was silent for a moment. "Look," she said at last, surprisingly, "I'm not usually such a bitch. Let's be friends, okay?" Her grin completely transformed her somewhat cynical expression. "It'll give Jamie and Ian fits, wondering what we're telling each other about them."

A reluctant smile tugged at Sarah's mouth, though she still felt wary. "That's two explicit offers of friendship I've had since I've been here," she said thoughtfully. "And the picture I'm getting of Jamie's life makes me think I'm going to need all the friends I can get."

FIDDLIN' FOOL • 121

Patsy nodded. "Who was the other offer?"

"Ian."

Patsy smiled. "He's not bad, is he? There are times when I think I could even stick with Ian."

She slid a potato and a peeler down the counter toward Sarah. "Here, you can help me. Otherwise I'll never finish."

Sarah slowly picked up the peeler. Shock was subsiding, but she still watched Patsy out of the corner of her eye, in case she attacked again.

Patsy's own gaze was fixed on her potato. "I'm actually a lot happier with Ian," she confided. "He takes me more seriously. Jamie's spectacular, and he likes everyone, but I never really have the feeling he's deeply involved. He always has that same good-natured detachment, if you know what I mean."

Sarah wasn't sure she did.

Sensing her disagreement, Patsy glanced at Sarah. "Maybe he's different with you." Sarah said nothing at first, but the two women looked at each other with the tentative beginnings of friendliness.

"I'd like to think so," Sarah said, "but I don't really know how involved he is."

Patsy sighed. "Ian, now, he's always involved." Her tone was ironic. "With everyone. And even if he weren't so emotionally promiscuous, I don't know what kind of a future we could have. Most of these Scottish and Irish musicians seem to stick to their own kind. They all marry other Celtic musicians."

Sarah felt as depressed at Patsy's observations as Patsy sounded.

"Well, it figures, doesn't it?" Patsy went on. "If you're a traditional musician, tradition must mean something to you, right? What's more unlikely than

122 · SUSAN RICHARDSON

a Scottish folk guitarist ending up with a jazz singer from Queens?"

Or a nursery-school teacher from California who's not even a musician? Sarah wondered.

"What about this Donald and Mary you mentioned?" she asked. "Are they from the same background?"

"No," Patsy replied. "Mary's Danish, actually. But then there are Alistair and Fiona and Colum and Lucy. They all practically grew up together. Guthrie, of course, is in love with himself."

"Ian seems fairly unconventional to me," Sarah said, trying to be reassuring.

"Hey, I don't care," Patsy claimed, her street-tough denial quick and instinctive. "I'm just generalizing. Personally, I think marriage is an anachronism. It doesn't matter to me what Ian does."

"Right," Sarah said emphatically, smiling. "Me neither. Couldn't care less."

Patsy shot her an indignant look. "Shut up and peel, *friend*," she said.

They both laughed, on the outside at least. Neither one of them was feeling all that optimistic inside.

Ten

Sarah swam slowly from sleep to consciousness, growing aware that someone was kissing her. There were light, feathery kisses over her temples, across her chin, down her jaw, and along her neck.

Ah! That tickled! She came fully awake with a giggle and raised her arms to place them around Jamie's neck.

"Good morning!" she murmured, turning to invite him to kiss her lips.

He chuckled as he rubbed his mouth back and forth against hers, but he didn't return her good morning. As his lips stopped their teasing and fastened on hers for his idea of a real kiss, her eyes suddenly flew open and her body stiffened in alarm.

It wasn't morning. It was dark outside! A bedside lamp lit one side of the room, but barely penetrated to the far corners. The windows were rectangles of blackness. It was nighttime. Quite late too.

She struggled to sit up. With a frustrated sigh

124 · SUSAN RICHARDSON

Jamie gave up the battle. He helped her to a sitting position.

"It's night," she gasped. He nodded, his expression implying that he was humoring a lunatic. "And I'm in Kentucky."

His eyes grew comically round. "Aye," he said. "In Luttrell Inn. On a bed. With a man named Jamie. Who hasn't seen you in three hours."

"Oh, shut up," she muttered, fully conscious now and feeling foolish. "It's grogginess I'm suffering from, not congenital idiocy."

"I'm relieved to hear it," he said, his gaze still lingering on her lips. But she was clearly not in a loving mood.

"When is the party?" she asked distractedly.

He shrugged. "In a while."

"Had I better dress for it?"

A roguish smile lit his face. "Aye. A good idea."

Sarah waited a moment until it became clear Jamie didn't intend to leave. "If you'll go," she hinted, "I'll wash up and get ready."

"I cannot leave you. You'd never find your way to the party."

"Jamie," she said threateningly.

He smiled at her and got up to cross to the closet. She watched in rising outrage as he rifled through her clothes and selected a pale-blue heavy cotton skirt printed with white clouds and a matching blue knit shirt.

"Here," he said, tossing the outfit on the bed. "You look like a summer day in this."

"Jamie, I am not changing my clothes with you in here!"

He seated himself in a chair near the door and leaned back with arms crossed to enjoy the show.

FIDDLIN' FOOL • 125

"Why not?" he asked reasonably. "Are you planning to reveal something I haven't seen before?"

She glared at him. She wasn't too shy to change in front of Jamie. But she didn't trust him not to touch her while she was dressing. And if he touched her, they might make love. Right now, in a strange place, surrounded by strangers, and with Patsy's disturbing words still fresh in her mind, she wouldn't feel comfortable making love with Jamie.

"Someone will come," she said desperately.

"Aye, likely they will soon enough," he agreed. "You'd best hurry then, hadn't you?"

Her chest rose and fell in agitation. She put her hands on her hips in an effort to look threatening.

"My nerves are never going to hold out here," she said in a vain attempt to arouse his sympathy.

"Ach, it's all a matter of practice. You'll find you get braver with exposure to someone like myself." He flashed a taunting grin.

"Crazier, you mean!"

Sighing with exasperated defeat, Sarah stomped to the wardrobe for clean underwear. Then she quickly and brusquely stripped to her teddy, a frivolous thing she'd bought in a moment's madness between two of Jamie's trips, when she was missing him. She kicked off her low-heeled pumps and marched to the small mirror-topped sink.

With quick businesslike movements she filled the sink with cool water and bent over to splash her face. Surfacing, she reached for a folded towel and dabbed the water out of her eyes. As she looked up, she saw Jamie's reflection in the mirror.

He wasn't smiling any longer. In fact his mouth was tight, as if he were suppressing pain.

Two things happened to Sarah. A sense of power

126 • SUSAN RICHARDSON

combined with her anger at him to suggest that two could play this teasing game. Why should he be the only one to dish it out? Let him squirm a bit.

The second thing to happen was that a warmth spread throughout her body, making it easy and natural to slow and smooth her movements. Pretending to ignore Jamie, she reached into her overnight case for hairpins. She wound thick fistfuls of her hair into a knot and secured it casually on top of her head. Then she squeezed a thoughtfully provided sponge into the water and, lifting and arching her neck, stroked and sponged herself. She half-turned so that she could see Jamie in the mirror and he had a profile view of her.

Jamie was definitely in pain. As Sarah's arm lifted and fell and reached, her body shifted with grace and symmetry. She moved sensuously, her eyes closed as she gave herself to the experience of cool water and rough sponge. Jamie shifted in his chair, trying to alleviate his discomfort and release some of the unbearable tension he was feeling.

Sarah herself was finding a curious pleasure in the game. She had begun it to punish Jamie, but his reaction had turned her into warm butter. As she slipped one strap down to sponge a breast, she heard a low, hoarse, continuous stream of what had to be Gaelic curses coming from Jamie. Startled out of her sensuous reverie, she turned to see him coming toward her. A little thrill of alarm shot through her when she read the intention clearly written on his face.

"Jamie . . . not now."

"To hell with that," he said harshly, reaching for her.

The hand she put out to stop him held the dripping sponge. It came into squishing contact with his clean blue shirt.

She gasped and he yelped as the cool water soaked the shirt. Backing up, he looked down at the Rorschach blot. Sarah was biting her lip guiltily, but her mouth was twitching with humor.

"Water again!" Jamie muttered explosively. Then they were both laughing helplessly, staggering about the room with their arms around each other.

"You wouldn't be a Pisces, would you?" Jamie asked.

As their laughter died, he said, "I'll have to go change."

She nodded. "Aye, you'd best do so."

He shot her a glinting look from narrowed eyes. "I'll be right back for the rest of the show. Wait for me!"

She tilted her head tauntingly, her brows raised, indicating that she might or might not.

When Jamie returned, Sarah was sitting fully clothed at the dressing table, her hair combed and rewound in a loose chignon, and was lightly applying the eyeliner that was her only makeup.

Jamie didn't knock, and as he opened the door he was still talking over his shoulder to some companions in the hall.

"Gargle with salt water, then," he was saying. "You're the only real singer here so far. You can't get out of it."

Sarah's lips tightened as he closed the door and walked toward her. Why didn't he just paste a sign on her door: "Jamie's Woman's Room"?

The little scene activated her prickly pride, so that when Jamie said, "Let's go, then," she replied coolly, "Go ahead. I'll be down when I'm ready."

128 • SUSAN RICHARDSON

"Don't be silly," he said. "You're coming with me."

She gasped in outrage and all her pent-up emotions boiled over into anger. She whirled on the stool to face him.

"You don't own me!" she said in a choked voice. Her eyes flashed and her cheeks flew flags of bright color. "Right now I'm not even sure if I like you."

Jamie grinned, ignoring her furious outburst. He'd been expecting something of this sort. He recognized that being alone here and dependent on him in some sense would make Sarah want to show him that she didn't need him and wasn't dancing to his tune. Wasn't just another Patsy, or something.

He studied her. Her expression was still tight and hostile. No sign of relenting. He bent over and kissed her, swiftly and hard. That did change her expression. She was startled and unsure now.

His smile was warm. He bent to kiss her again, lingeringly, until he felt her mouth soften and start to respond.

He did own her, Sarah thought as she gave herself over to the inevitable attraction of his kiss. At least he owned her body's responses. She could no more resist him than fly. He could make her forget where she was, what she was doing, who was likely to appear at any moment, what her name was. Never, as long as she lived, would she be able to escape her response to him.

As he reluctantly drew away from her, he put his hands on her shoulders. "Sarah," he said gently, "there's nothing I'd like better than a fight with you." His voice lowered intimately. "And its inevitable aftermath."

Her eyes sparked, but she didn't contradict him. She, too, knew how that encounter would end.

"But we haven't the time," he continued, "so would you please, pretty please, come with me now? I don't want to tell you what to do, but I do want to introduce you to my friends myself."

She couldn't resist the smile or the gentleness. She nodded. He held a hand down to her and helped her to her feet. They crossed the room together. At the door, he said, "That's my girl," and slapped her gently on the bottom. It was a mistake, he realized.

She smiled sweetly and motioned him out first. As he passed her, she swung her arm back and returned his slap to the bottom, not so gently. "That's my boy," she said challengingly.

He chuckled as he turned to encounter her cheery, innocent smile. "You little devil!" he said admiringly.

"You chauvinistic Hebridean pig!" she replied lovingly.

Then she giggled, her ill humor all worked out.

They walked down the hall together, arm in arm and in perfect accord.

At the top of the stairs they heard voices from below. Sarah suddenly became aware that she was on the edge of an ordeal she'd dreaded for days. She had been so absorbed in her private battle with Jamie, it had crept up on her.

Downstairs were the friends and colleagues whose doubtful acceptance meant so much to her. All the people who were closest to Jamie and with whom he had so much in common—heritage, skills, livelihood, shared experiences—and to whom she would be just another woman Jamie had brought along.

He felt her hesitation and glanced down at her. She appeared calm and composed. Only a slight quivering of the mouth betrayed her apprehension, and no one who didn't know her would notice it.

130 · SUSAN RICHARDSON

Her head was high and her shoulders squared. She was a gallant little thing.

Feeling his gaze, she looked up and flashed him a quick smile. He smiled reassuringly in return, and she turned her head resolutely to the front again. They descended.

It wasn't so bad. There weren't more than twenty-five people in the big, empty ballroom, and some of them were local, so Jamie didn't know them either. And Jamie's friends were a friendly, informal lot— bordering on outrageous.

She met Donald and Mary. Donald was tall and cadaverous and very funny. Mary was smooth and blond and beautiful, with a lovely serenity about her. Sarah felt she could have another friend there.

She and Jamie both met for the first time various members of the television crew. They would be coming and going for the next two weeks as they filmed for the Public Communications Network documentary on the making of the festival.

Guthrie was there, of course, the heart and soul of the party. He cheerfully ordered everyone around and took unashamed credit for the refreshments Venetta had prepared, to the vast disgust of Ian, who had led Patsy up to them.

"If he lives out the month, it'll be a miracle," Ian muttered to Jamie and Sarah when he and Patsy joined them. "George'll kill him if I don't."

"Mary and I have a bet on which day violence will first break out," Patsy said in her low, cynical voice.

Jamie chuckled. "Hello, Patsy," he said casually. "You're looking fine." She was wearing black again, Sarah noticed, but this time it was satin.

Patsy tilted her head and pursed her lips as she looked assessingly back at Jamie.

FIDDLIN' FOOL · 131

Sarah was watching the meeting carefully, nerves as tight as a piano wire. She almost jumped when Ian draped his arm across her shoulders in a friendly gesture. "We'll just let them get it over with, shall we?" he whispered into Sarah's ear. She returned a wry smile.

"And you're as gorgeous as ever, Jamie," Patsy drawled. "But you've finally found a lady who up-stages you." She nodded and smiled at Sarah, who nodded back. "Was that good theater?"

Jamie looked half resigned, half pained, like a good boy taking his medicine. "Wouldn't you rather just hit me?" he suggested.

Patsy grinned. "No, I'm finished now. I took the rest of it out on Sarah this afternoon." Her grin widened at Jamie's raised eyebrows. She winked at Sarah as she detached Ian from her. "Come on, Ian, there's music. Let's dance and get this party started."

Sarah studied Jamie's face, but it didn't tell her a lot. He watched Patsy and Ian go with resigned amusement, then turned to her.

"We'll dance, too, shall we?" he said, and tugged her into his arms. His gaze was direct and unapologetic, but perhaps a bit wary. "So you've met Patsy already, have you?"

"Yes," Sarah said brightly, following his strong lead automatically. "She says you're very good in bed. But then, I already knew that."

He swung her around abruptly, swearing under his breath and rolling his eyes. She caught something that sounded like "cursed troublemaker."

"She probably is," Sarah said equably, "but I like her anyway." She was proud of how detached she sounded.

Jamie felt a spurt of surprise that she was taking

132 • SUSAN RICHARDSON

it so well. "That's the worst of Patsy," he said. "You can't really dislike her."

Sarah said nothing for a moment as they danced, struggling to hang on to that detachment. But she couldn't leave the subject. "Am I likely to meet any others?" she asked, hoping she sounded light and casual. "Because I would prefer to be prepared next time."

Jamie let out an explosive breath. He should have known it wouldn't be that easy. "What do you take me for?" he asked.

"I don't know what to take you for," she said in a reasonable, slightly unsteady voice. "That's what I'm trying to find out." She could feel the detachment slipping away. She hadn't had a very good grip on it anyhow.

Jamie wasn't looking at her. He was looking over her head at nothing in particular, but his expression was grim. "Look," he bit out, "what happened before I met you doesn't concern you."

Her eyes rounded in amazement. "This is purely a one-dimensional relationship, is it?" she asked hotly. "For the moment only? Neither one of us to know anything about the other's past or think about the future? Is that what you mean?"

He removed his hand from her waist to run it impatiently through his hair, then replaced it more firmly than was necessary. "No, that's not what I mean!"

There was a silence. "All right," he conceded finally, as if Sarah had been arguing. "I suppose I'm just annoyed at having this happen at all. It seems so irrelevant, somehow. What happened with Patsy is over, and in terms of importance it isn't even in

FIDDLIN' FOOL · 133

the same universe with what's happening between you and me."

"Well, that's very nice, I suppose," Sarah said slowly, "but at the risk of seeming petty and prying, I'd like to point out that if I'm going to be spending time with you and Patsy and Ian, I'd prefer not to spend it wondering what's behind Patsy's barbed comments."

Jamie smiled faintly. "You have a point there, I suppose. All right. Let's talk pasts. Were you imagining my group of friends consisted of a set of revolving couples hitting any convenient bed between rehearsals?"

"Of course not!" she said, but the color in her face betrayed that she had been thinking along those lines.

He grinned. "Liar," he said gently. "Well, I'm sorry to disappoint you, but we're all fairly dull, hard-working fellows. Our night life is spent onstage, for the most part."

Her chin jutted out stubbornly. She refused to feel foolish for wanting information about the situation she'd been catapulted into.

Jamie's grin faded. "There were women, of course," he said abruptly. He was finding the whole conversation distasteful and wanted to get it over with. "I'm a man, not a eunuch. But it was occasional and casual. I've never had time for a serious relationship. Patsy was a friend and a business associate, to begin with. She's part owner of a club I play in in New York. We were spending a lot of time together anyway. I suppose that's how it happened and why it continued. But it didn't mean as much to me as it did to her. When I realized that, I cut it off. That was shortly before I met you. I suppose I did it callously,

134 • SUSAN RICHARDSON

or too abruptly, or something, and that's why she's so angry."

Sarah didn't think that was why Patsy was angry, but she'd heard enough. In fact, maybe too much. She felt silly for having staged this sordid little scene. Maybe she was too much the conventional little suburbanite to handle what was, after all, just real life. Jamie's annoyance was justified. What right did she have to put him on the spot and demand explanations? She was acting like a jealous wife. And she felt like a fool.

She shot a quick look up at his face and felt that she was letting him down badly. He'd brought her along expecting an adult companion, and here she was behaving like an insecure child.

She reached up to touch his face lightly. He looked down at her questioningly. "I'm sorry," she murmured. "As Patsy says, 'I'm all through being a bitch.' It's out of my system. I didn't mean to grill you."

"It's all right," he said with chagrin. "Now I'll apologize. I should have realized how all this would look to you. But Sarah, you mustn't think musicians are all that much different from other folk. A bit more dramatic, perhaps, in dress or manners. But it's just like any other crowd, really." He was very serious.

"Oh, I know, I know," she said quickly and earnestly. "Really I do. I'm sorry. I was just being provincial."

He grinned. "Once more around the circle and we can quit. 'I'm sorry, I'm sorry, you're sorry, you're sorry.' There. All finished."

She smiled wanly, but humiliation kept her from quite meeting Jamie's eyes. He looked at her thoughtfully, and they finished the dance in silence.

When the music ended, voices clamored for Jamie

to "give us a tune, lad." "Show us what you've learned on yer travels."

Jamie slanted Sarah a questioning look. "Will you be okay?" it asked.

She nodded firmly, only too eager to show Jamie she wasn't an insecure, possessive woman. His gaze searched her face. Apparently reassured, he squeezed her hand and left.

While Jamie tuned his fiddle, Sarah made her way to Mary and Patsy, who had also been abandoned by men fetching instruments. Patsy grinned at her like a defiant bad child.

"You're having all kinds of fun today, aren't you, Patsy?" Sarah said, smiling wryly.

Patsy laughed.

Mary looked at her with weary tolerance. "It's a kind of testing," she said to Sarah. "Patsy feels that only the people who put up with her tongue are true friends."

Patsy laughed again, but she looked uncomfortable. Sarah had an idea that Mary's remark had hit fairly close to home.

After playing a lively gavotte from Brittany, Jamie called, "Guthrie, bring up your whistles. Ian, I need a guitar." Donald was there with his accordion, too, and the camera crew was sprinting for equipment. This impromptu concert would provide great footage.

Soon everyone in the room was swaying and stomping and shouting and whistling. No one could resist the music, and the party took off, half concert, half dance. Sarah found herself whirled around the room in one set of arms or another as Jamie played on and on. His face was alight with the joy of the music and the camaraderie onstage.

Between numbers, Sarah talked with various peo-

136 · SUSAN RICHARDSON

ple. She was determined to make her own place here and her own friendships. Once Jamie nodded approvingly at her when he heard her laugh, and she stiffened instinctively. So what if she had felt shaky earlier? she thought. He needn't be patronizing! She lifted her chin and ostentatiously turned her back on him.

Ian and Jamie had paused between tunes to sip their drinks. Ian watched as Jamie's gaze followed Sarah around the room, and he noted Jamie's glum expression.

"Yon Sarah's something a bit special, isn't she?" he probed with the frankness of an old friend.

"Aye," Jamie replied laconically, tossing back his head to finish off his drink.

"You'd best take her with you when you go home," Ian said.

Jamie snorted. "So far, she's not mad about the life. Thinks we're a loose bunch."

"Ah, you underestimate her. She's no buttoned-up puritan."

"No," Jamie agreed, "but she's skittish. I don't know if I can hold her. You've never seen anyone run for cover so fast. And half the time I don't even know why."

"She wouldn't be here if she had runnin' in mind."

"If she's still here at the end of the two weeks, I'll maybe think I've got a chance with her," Jamie said gloomily.

Ian snorted in disgust. "Ach, pick up yer fiddle, man, and talk with that if you can't make better sense with yer mouth. The girl's mad for you."

It was a couple of hours after midnight when Jamie left the other musicians on the stage to seek

FIDDLIN' FOOL • 137

out Sarah. He found her leaning against a wall, alone for the moment, an empty glass in her hand.

"Shall I refill that for you?" he asked.

"No, I'm going up. I'm tired. Are you coming?"

He shook his head reluctantly. "I've got to talk to the film director about shots of tomorrow's rehearsals. But I'll walk you up."

At the door of her room he reached for her. With a sigh she relaxed against his broad chest and wrapped her arms around him.

Under her ear she heard his rich voice say, "You were a great success tonight, you know. It's rare for a nonmusician to receive this kind of welcome. But then, I knew you'd charm them all silly."

The pride and pleasure in his voice were unmistakable. And was there, Sarah mused, also a tinge of relief?

Out of nowhere came a sudden resentment. It was because she was so tired, she tried to tell herself. She wasn't feeling sensible. But the thought refused to go away. He'd said, "You were a great success." Not "the *ceilidh* was a great success," or "the meeting was a success." Was she on trial, then? she wondered. Of course she'd known and accepted his doubts about her suitability to his life. She hadn't minded before. Why now? Why the resentment? Was it because she was doubting herself?

She allowed herself to be held and kissed good night. And while her body responded, as it always would with Jamie, for the first time her emotions remained unengaged. She felt like a puppet moving to someone else's command.

After the kiss Jamie held her at arm's length, his gaze searching her face. Insensitivity was not one of

138 • SUSAN RICHARDSON

his failings. He knew she was still holding back, and there wasn't a damn thing he could do about it.

"Good night, Sarah," he said quietly.

"Good night."

He was still looking at her, and Sarah had the feeling he was waiting for something. When she said nothing else, he nodded and left her.

She lay awake for a long time wondering if Jamie would come that night and wondering, if he did, if she could welcome him as though nothing were wrong.

But there wasn't anything wrong, was there? she asked herself. No, she answered, there wasn't. She was being silly. She just would like another day to get over this feeling before she and Jamie made love again.

When she finally fell asleep, realizing she was going to get her wish, she couldn't have explained why she felt none of the relief she would have expected, but just a vast, aching emptiness.

Eleven

Sarah looked up from the notebook in which she'd been scribbling for hours. She had wanted to get down on paper some of the characters she'd met in the past few days.

It was time to shift her position. Her shady spot above the inn had long since moved on, and it was no day to be sitting in the bright sun. It was hot—low nineties—with a thick, humid heat that left her feeling limp if she didn't protect herself against it.

She would move in a minute, she decided, sighing and stretching her stiff back. She looked with deep contentment at the inn and the sparkling river below her, and around at the green hills on all sides. She couldn't believe she'd been here a week already.

It had been a happy week, for the most part. Every day she felt more a part of the expanding group of musicians and television people. She sat in on rehearsals, ran errands for the film crew, helped Venetta and Patsy with the cooking, and roamed the hills, sometimes alone, sometimes with one of her newfound

139

140 • SUSAN RICHARDSON

friends. She couldn't get over the beauty of the lush green woods and mossy creekbeds, so different from California's golden summer-baked hills.

The inn was filling. Not all the performers would come early, but only those who were leading workshops, or who needed rehearsal time as ensembles or duos formed solely for this event. Other groups and solo performers would be arriving the day before the festival.

Still, it seemed like a crowd already. The inn had lost that bare, lonely quality. Now it rang with shouts and laughter and snatches of music around the clock.

The only blot on the week, Sarah reflected, was that Jamie was so busy. She felt they'd actually grown farther apart rather than closer, as she'd hoped.

He came to her room most nights, usually hours after she'd gone to bed, and pulled her close while he snatched a few hours of sleep. A couple of times they'd made love, taking and giving pleasure in the early morning hours with a sleepy warmth that left Sarah unsure whether or not she'd dreamed it.

During the day it was a quick smile or a wave from the distance, an occasional squeeze of the hand in passing. Jamie seemed to be handling everything well, but it was a killing pace, even for him, and the strain showed. There was an edge to his voice for the first time since Sarah had known him. More often than not it had to do with Guthrie.

"Jamie," Guthrie would complain, "I simply cannot play with that insensitive Ian Grant thumping along in the background. I could stamp my foot with more rhythm than he provides."

"Guthrie, if you complain to me once more about Ian, I'm going to give him permission to kill you. I'll

FIDDLIN' FOOL • 141

go so far as to provide him with an alibi." It was said with a smile, but even Jamie's sense of humor was wearing thin.

Recognizing the pressure Jamie was under, Sarah was determined not to add to it. She wanted in the worst way to grab him and hold on, yet she forced herself to let go.

She wouldn't be like the others, she told herself, like the singer, Peggy, who rubbed up against him every time they talked together. Touching him meant too much to her; it had too much of an emotional charge.

As hard as she tried to be tolerant and open-minded, Sarah had difficulty with the casual affection of so many of the musicians. It bothered her to see Jamie with Peggy's arm around his waist, or Carly Stewart sitting in his lap. She could feel herself withdrawing in reaction. Was Patsy right about Jamie's habit of detachment? she wondered. How much did their lovemaking mean to him?

She was startled out of her thoughts by Patsy's faint voice calling from below. "Hello, up there! Can you abandon the creative muse for a minute?"

Sarah smiled and got to her feet, brushing at the grass stains on her shorts. "Coming," she called, and began to make her way down the path to the foot of the cliff.

Patsy was waiting, hands on her hips. "Did I interrupt a masterpiece?" she asked irreverently.

"I was ready for a break anyway," Sarah said calmly. She was used to Patsy's jibes by now. "What's up?"

"Ian and I are going into town. Want to come?"

Sarah glanced at her watch. "Can Venetta do supper without us?"

"She says she can. So how about it?"

142 · *SUSAN RICHARDSON*

Sarah's impulse was to say no thanks. Then she realized she was hoping for a chance to see Jamie if she stuck around. Don't be a drip, she told herself fiercely, waiting around hoping for a crumb of attention!

"Sure," she said, determinedly cheerful. "Give me a minute to change?"

"We'll meet you at the garage. Fifteen minutes, okay?"

Patsy left to find Ian, and Sarah was climbing the steps to the veranda when Jamie came out the front door.

Her heart contracted and she couldn't help but smile at the sight of him. He had circles under his eyes and circles of perspiration under the arms of his blue shirt. He needed a shave. But his eyes were crinkled in a warm smile for her, and even exhausted he radiated twice the vitality of most people. There would never be a time when he looked less than perfect to her.

"There you are," he said. "I was looking for you."

"You were?" She felt absurdly pleased.

He nodded, walking over to her. "There's an ensemble rehearsal coming up that should be close to good. Will you come?"

He put his hands on her shoulders to make the invitation more persuasive. He wanted her to come, he thought as he studied her face, even if it meant only that they'd be sitting in the same room together. He felt he'd hardly seen her these last few days, and his frustration was building. True, he was busy and he should be glad she'd found friends. But whenever he was free, she was nowhere around. Looking up at him with her clear-eyed gaze and in shorts that showed the shapely length of her legs,

FIDDLIN' FOOL • 143

she wasn't helping his dedication to his work. Maybe they could slip off together after the rehearsal. . . .

She shook her head. "I can't," she said sadly. "I'm going into town with Patsy and Ian." She wanted in the worst way to say yes, but that would be weak, wouldn't it?

A quick frown passed over Jamie's face. "Why do I never see you anymore?" he asked.

Sarah felt a spark of annoyance. "What do you mean?" she countered, more sharply that she intended. "You're the one who's always busy. Am I supposed to just twiddle my thumbs and wait until you can disentangle yourself from your many admirers and crook your little finger for me?"

His eyes narrowed. "So that's it. How long are you going to punish me for Patsy?"

Sarah gasped. "What are you talking about? I'm not punishing you for anything!"

"What then?" he asked. "Why are you never around?"

Rage was building in Sarah. How dare he act as if he were the aggrieved party? "I'm just enjoying myself," she said flatly, but her eyes were flashing.

Jamie nodded grimly. "Ah, I see. The party's proving more of an attraction than the man."

"I don't believe this!" She stared up at his belligerent face. Then, in a quieter voice, she said, "And you don't believe that."

She watched as he struggled with himself—honesty versus frustration. His mouth twisted in self-mockery and he lowered his head until his forehead touched hers. "Perhaps I don't," he said. Irony threaded his voice as he added, "Do you suppose Guthrie's winning the battle for my sanity?"

She chuckled and slid her arms around his waist. They stood like that for a few minutes, experiencing

144 · SUSAN RICHARDSON

the relief of having averted a quarrel. Then Jamie said, "Are you sure I can't change your mind about staying here this afternoon?"

Before Sarah could answer, a car came into sight around the bend in the road, drawing their attention. They lifted their heads and watched as it pulled up to the foot of the steps and a handsome man with dark curly hair jumped out.

"Jamie!" he called out in an Irish accent, slamming the car door behind him. "It's yourself. And fondling a beautiful woman as usual."

Jamie felt Sarah's shoulders hunch. His own expression was sardonic.

Undaunted, the Irishman continued with his flood of musical speech as he briskly climbed the steps. "I loved your new album, man. You're makin' life difficult for the rest of us with the standards you're settin'. And introduce me to the lovely lady here. Where have you been hidin' this one?" His blue eyes flashed boldly at her.

Jamie turned Sarah so that she, too, faced the Irishman, but he kept his hands on her shoulders. "Sarah," he said, "this smooth-talking fellow is Liam O'Neil. Next to Ian, he's the man I'd most have you stay away from."

Liam received this with a shout of laughter, head thrown back to reveal gleaming white teeth.

Reluctantly, Jamie added, "Liam, this is Sarah Hughes. She's . . . mine." He knew as soon as he said it that the words were a mistake. He'd meant, hands off. But judging by the tightening of her mouth, she'd taken it quite another way.

In Sarah's current state of uncertainty about Jamie's feelings, nothing could have more surely hurt her than those words. "She's . . . mine." She read the hesitation as meaning that Jamie didn't know how to categorize her—my woman, my mistress —so had just settled for *mine.*

Humiliation burned in her. She was no man's possession, especially not a man who granted no reciprocal rights.

"Actually, I'm my own," she said sweetly, putting out her hand to Liam in greeting.

Jamie silently cursed himself.

With a brilliant smile Sarah continued. "I'm happy to meet you, but you'll have to excuse me. Patsy and Ian are waiting for me."

"You won't stay?" Jamie asked in a low voice.

She avoided his eyes. "No, it's already arranged," she said firmly, stepping away from him. "Can I bring you anything from town?"

"A bottle of Glenfiddich," he muttered.

Liam was observing the two of them with bright interest. "See you later," Sarah said to him, and whisked inside without a glance for Jamie.

A muscle twitched in Jamie's cheek as he watched her go. Everything that happened between them seemed to widen the gap that had grown that first day here. Couldn't he do anything right? he asked himself in disgust.

He shoved his hands into his pockets and stomped into the inn himself, leaving Liam abandoned on the veranda with his eyebrows raised to his hairline.

Sarah got back late that night, and for once Jamie was asleep before her. She stood at the side of the bed looking down at him. One arm was flung up limply beside his unshaven cheek, and the lines of exhaustion were etched clearly on his craggy face.

She was remembering his words from this after-

146 · SUSAN RICHARDSON

noon. Did he really want to see more of her? She smiled at the thought. Perhaps she had gone overboard with this independent stance. If he wanted to be with her, and heaven knows she wanted to be with him, it seemed a little silly to be always saving face.

Tomorrow, if he had time for her, she'd be there. He had invited her here, after all. He must want to spend some time with her.

She watched his bare chest rise and fall with his breathing. She ached to touch him, to smooth his fair hair and caress his eyelids. But he looked so tired. And there was a strong odor of whisky in the room.

Perhaps that was why he didn't even move when she slid between the sheets and snuggled close to offer what comfort she could. Or was she just seeking it for herself?

Sarah was helping Venetta and Patsy prepare breakfast the next morning, when Jamie entered the kitchen, looking like death.

"Good morning," Sarah said cheerily.

"Shhhh," he replied. He slid into a chair and rested his head on his hands.

"Too much drinking?" she asked with scant sympathy

"And what else is there to do in the evenings around here?" he demanded. "Ian appropriates all the female companionship. The rest of us do the best we can."

Venetta placed a cup of tea at Jamie's elbow. "Here," she said, failing to keep the amusement out of her voice. "Have a cup of tea."

He looked up at her with one eye closed. "Where's

the sympathy that's supposed to come with it?" he asked.

"How's this?" Patsy offered. " 'You poor fool.' "

He sipped his tea gingerly. "Not quite what I had in mind," he muttered, "but you can spare yourselves further strenuous efforts if you'll lend me Sarah for the morning."

Sarah leaned against the big old metal sink, a tender smile on her face as she watched Jamie drink his tea with his eyes closed. He was pale, almost gray. His eyes when they were open were bloodshot. He was beautiful.

"Can you do without Sarah for a while, Venetta?" he asked.

"Well, yes," Venetta said with gentle humor, "seeing as how everything's all ready anyway."

Jamie stood—carefully—and looked with approval at Sarah. She apparently had intended to walk that morning, he thought, since she was wearing her hiking boots. In dark green jeans and a light green T-shirt, she looked like sea foam and sunlight. He wouldn't promise to keep his hands off her today.

She set down her teacup and took the hand he held out to her. "Where are we going?" she asked.

"Off," he replied firmly. "Far off. It's too long since I had you to myself."

She sighed contentedly, and he smiled. He'd had all he could stand of watching her from a distance, stuffing his hands into his pockets to keep them under control. He was feeling better by the second just with the prospect of spending time with her.

"Are you hungry, Sarah?" Patsy asked. "Shall I pack you something to eat? Or are you going to live on love today?"

148 • SUSAN RICHARDSON

Jamie answered for her. "Love," he said, unabashed by Patsy's cynical teasing.

Sarah and Jamie both had the urge just to go, unencumbered. They walked down to the river, past the inn's gardens and the tennis courts, hand in hand.

Jamie was dressed for hiking himself, in sturdy boots and his usual jeans and shirt. He screwed up his eyes as he scanned the morning sky, assessing the chances of rain. Sarah watched him, thinking how automatic the gesture seemed. Every islander must check the sky as a matter of course each morning, she thought.

She looked up herself, trying to read something in the fleecy clouds moving briskly overhead. Air currents. And beautiful fresh air. Exhilarating breezes. That was all she got. Jamie was watching her in amusement. "Rain likely?" he teased.

She tossed her head. "You tell me. You're the country boy."

"Well, if this weather holds another week, we'll be lucky. It's always risky scheduling an outdoor concert."

They walked along swinging hands for a bit, neither one feeling any need to talk.

Near the path that led into the woods, Jamie said in a pleased voice, "It's wonderful how the crowd here has taken to you. You even have Patsy begging to fix you little tidbits." He shook his head in disbelief. "I can't think of anyone else who's won acceptance so quickly in this group."

Sarah's smile disappeared as if it had been erased from a chalkboard. Anger shook her, so strongly that she had no control over it for a moment. Silently and coldly she pulled her hand from Jamie's,

FIDDLIN' FOOL • 149

not even bothering to pretend she needed to brush her hair out of her eyes or some such thing. Would she never be through passing tests? she wondered. How many other people had to accept her before Jamie was prepared to?

Jamie looked down at her averted face, his eyes narrowing and a muscle clenching in his jaw. Now what? She was always pulling away from him these days. She had more warmth for Patsy and Ian than she did for him. What went on in her head?

They continued walking, but the silence was tense now, no longer companionable. Sarah was hanging on to her anger to keep from crying. Above all, she didn't want to cry.

Finally they reached a clearing surrounded and shielded from view by mountain laurels. It was warm and sunny there.

Jamie dropped to the ground and pulled Sarah down to sit beside him. She allowed herself to be coaxed down, but she turned slightly away from him, bending her legs up and resting her head on arms folded atop her knees.

He watched her for a moment, looking for a sign of warmth and getting seduced by the way the sun reflected off her hair and skin. He reached for the fat braid in which she'd tried to confine her hair and tugged gently to encourage her to move closer to him.

"No, Jamie," she said coolly.

Her coolness lit a flame of anger in him.

He rose to a sitting position, then took her arm and pulled her off balance. He rolled so that he was lying on top of her.

"No!" she said sharply.

150 • SUSAN RICHARDSON

"Yes," he said. "I want you. And I'm getting sick of being pushed away."

It probably wouldn't have happened if she hadn't pulled her hand from his earlier, or if he hadn't had too much to drink the night before. But a slow panic was rising in him. He felt she was slipping away, and his fear urged him to cover her lips with his insistent ones, ignoring her attempt to turn her head.

Just be still, he pleaded silently. Stop running. Let it happen, Sarah. It was nearly an instinct with him to halt her. She was constantly on the edge of flight, he felt, like a bird. If he let go of her, she would fly away and never come back.

He felt her resistance ebb before a strangled sob forced its way out against his mouth. He raised his head in instant concern. "Sarah," he asked helplessly, "what is it?"

She was crying, her eyes closed, tears rolling out from between the lids. Finally she choked out, "Oh, Jamie, I'm so afraid."

Remorse shook him to his foundation. He could have groveled at her feet, begging forgiveness. Groaning deep in his throat, he pressed his face to the ground beside her head.

"Dear Lord, Sarah! I'm so sorry. Never again. You have to believe me. Never. I don't know what I was doing. Please. Don't be afraid of me."

At the sound of his aghast voice, Sarah opened her eyes. He thought she was afraid of him. It hadn't occurred to her. If there was anything in life she was sure of, it was that Jamie would never hurt her. The fear that was fueling her resistance was different. It was a fear of loving him so much and giving so much of herself to him, there might not be anything left when he went away. At every hint of a reservation on his part, her instinct was to withdraw to a safe place, to leave before she was left.

She felt his anguish in the tension of his body, and she knew the shame he had to be feeling now. What she didn't know was how to say that it wasn't him she was afraid of. She couldn't tell him that she dreaded leaving him without making him feel bound to her. So she said nothing.

He started to roll off her, but she restrained him with a gentle hand. She couldn't tell him, but she couldn't let him go like this.

He looked at her in anguish.

"It's all right, Jamie," she said.

He shook his head, his eyes bleak. "No, it's not. I don't know if it'll ever be all right again."

She squeezed her eyes shut in pain. She was going to pretend he didn't say that, she told herself. She was going to have to pretend.

He stared at her face, not understanding the pain he read there. Didn't she know how ashamed he was? "Sarah?" he whispered at last.

"Just kiss me, Jamie," she begged.

Still trying to fathom her feelings, he kissed her, feeling his way, hoping his body could clear up the mess his mouth had made.

Beneath his lips hers trembled slightly, and he forced himself to concentrate on soothing and reassuring. Little, light kisses, soft as butterfly wings, all over her face. He tasted salt from her tears, and felt he could howl from the pain of hurting her.

She must remember to tell him she wasn't breakable, Sarah thought. But not today. Today she was feeling distinctly fragile. Today she hadn't the strength for passion.

152 • SUSAN RICHARDSON

Jamie drew away to look at her. Her eyes when they met his were wide, but less than open. Time, he thought. It would take some time for her to recover from this. Back off, you big clumsy buffalo, he told himself. See what happens when you pressure her?

Staring up at him, Sarah saw a strong man exercising strong restraint. She was letting him down again, she thought. He needs a woman; he needs the relaxation of uncomplicated loving. He needs someone who doesn't need so much from him that she's constantly aquiver with feelings. He doesn't need these constant tense confrontations.

He smiled and got to his feet, drawing her up with him. "Shall we walk some more?" he asked gently.

She nodded, determined to salvage something from this morning. Jamie pretended he didn't notice the bleakness behind her smile.

Twelve

The following week was bad for Sarah. As minimal as her nocturnal cuddles with Jamie had been, they were heaven compared to the current lonely nights. She had trouble sleeping, and her face took on the transparent look it got when she was sad and not eating well.

Jamie, when she saw him, was kind, friendly even, but in an almost impersonal way. He hadn't touched her since that day in the woods. She wouldn't have believed how much she could miss the casual hair rufflings or fleeting caresses on the shoulder in passing. She felt she'd even welcome a good-girl pat on the bottom these days.

He had lost interest, she decided one afternoon when she was helping Patsy in the kitchen. It wasn't surprising, really. She hadn't been tons of fun. Why should he go to the trouble of seeking her out when there were so many other women available?

She thought with a little spurt of despair of pretty

153

154 · SUSAN RICHARDSON

Peggy Keane and Carly Stewart, with her husky voice and dry wit.

The other day in the woods, she thought dully, when she had been so stiff must have put the seal on it. But if so, a stubborn voice in her mind pointed out, being together couldn't be for him what it was for her. She couldn't be what she wasn't. If she wasn't casual and flamboyant enough to fit into his life, she wasn't, that was all. And if he didn't care enough about her to make any sort of a commitment, then what difference did it make anyway?

Slowly she stopped shredding the lettuce for the salad as her gaze fixed unseeing on the opposite wall. Patsy, glancing up at that moment, did a double take and bit her lip in dismay at the grief on Sarah's face. She'd thought Sarah seemed a bit down lately, but this looked serious.

"Sarah," she asked bluntly, "what the hell is the matter with you?'

Sarah started guiltily. "Nothing," she said weakly.

"Don't give me that. You look like a half-drowned kitten. And it's not just you, come to think of it," she added, scowling suspiciously. "It's Jamie too. He's not the same old Jolly White Giant lately. He's downright nasty. Come on. Give. What's going on?"

"Nothing," Sarah said more forcefully, resuming work on the salad and avoiding Patsy's eyes. "You're imagining things. Putting this festival together is enough to make anyone nasty."

Patsy shook her head adamantly. "Not Jamie. I've seen him handle at least this much pressure with no more than a request for an extra drink. Certainly not any impairment of the perennial good humor. No. When I reach the point of feeling sorry for Guthrie, it's time to meddle."

FIDDLIN' FOOL • 155

Sarah smiled wanly. "At least you're honest."

"So follow Aunt Patsy's good example. A little honesty here, please."

Sarah looked at Patsy and, reading the concern behind her crusty manner, sagged. "Oh, Patsy," she said, tears flooding her eyes, "I think you were right about Jamie's detachment. He's kind, when he thinks of it, but things have gone wrong between us and he doesn't even seem to care. He hasn't been near me in days, and I botch things so badly—I'm so paranoid, or uptight, or whatever—when I do talk to him, it's almost a relief not to have to. I think I'd better just go home."

"Don't be stupid!" Patsy said with characteristic lack of tact. "Jamie's going around kicking Guthrie and other stray dogs because he doesn't care?" She was glad to see that Sarah could still smile. "He cares."

"Maybe he does. But it's just not working between us. And caring's not enough. At least not for what I want."

"Look," Patsy said, "if Jamie wanted it to end between you two, he'd tell you. Jamie's charming and good-natured for the most part, but it's because he feels like it, not for anyone else's benefit. He's more honest than kind. Believe me, I know. I *don't* know what's wrong between you two, but Jamie isn't feeling casual about it. That much I do know. So you're going nowhere!"

Sarah crossed her eyes and stuck out her tongue. Working with children had honed her facemaking talents. "Yes, your highness," she said sassily. "And when you figure out my lines for the next scene, don't forget to give me a copy of the script." She

156 • SUSAN RICHARDSON

didn't believe anything Patsy said. Strange that it should make her feel so much better.

"I won't," Patsy promised.

"Ian," Patsy said later when the opportunity presented itself, "something's wrong between Jamie and Sarah, and Sarah's pining."

Ian shot her a sharp look. "Are you sure you're not a wee bit glad about that?" he asked.

Patsy looked at him in blank astonishment before his meaning penetrated. Then she smiled knowingly as she moved closer and languidly draped her arms around his neck.

"What would I want with Jamie now that I've finally gotten your attention?" she purred.

Ian's scowl dissolved into a silly smile.

Several minutes later he lifted his head to breathe, and was still smiling.

Patsy, through her own cocky grin, said, "We'll have to do something about Sarah and Jamie. Neither one of them has enough sense to deal with this."

"Aye, all right. I'll be havin' a word with the fair-haired boyo. Later. Right now I have a few words for you alone."

It was the next day, the day of the opening concert of the festival, before Ian got his chance. He found Jamie alone in the kitchen, wolfing down a sandwich.

"So you do eat," Ian said, turning a chair so he could straddle it, his arms crossed on its back.

Jamie made an inarticulate sound.

"I've been wantin' to talk to you," Ian went on.

"Umm?" Jamie muttered, still chewing, his eyebrows raised.

FIDDLIN' FOOL • 157

"It's about Sarah."

Jamie swallowed abruptly. "What about Sarah?" he demanded.

"She's sufferin', that's what. Why don't you talk to the girl? What are yer intentions toward her?"

Jamie exploded. "What do you think they are?"

"I don't know," Ian said, unmoved by his friend's outburst. "And no more does she."

"Of course she knows," Jamie said unequivocably. "She just doesn't share my intentions."

Ian simply shook his head. "She doesn't know."

Jamie ran his hand through his hair in exasperation. "Would I have brought her here if I intended anything but getting her to marry me?"

Again Ian shrugged, this time more elaborately. "Who knows? Haven't you always made yer own rules?"

Ian let Jamie scowl at the table for a moment before he added, "Sarah thinks you wanted a light affair."

Jamie looked up, his lower lip jutting out belligerently. "You're daft."

Ian shook his head. "Patsy says so."

With barely controlled impatience, Jamie waved a hand dismissingly. "You're not fool enough to take Patsy's word on this," he said scornfully.

Ian, who had patiently endured Jamie's bad temper, stood up, scraping his chair across the flagstone floor. "Aye, I am," he said with quiet fierceness. "Because she's not in love with you anymore; she's in love with me. And you know as well as I do that Patsy's not one to stick knives in backs. She'll blast you to yer face, but she'll never do an underhanded thing." He stared uncompromisingly at Jamie through narrowed eyes.

158 · SUSAN RICHARDSON

Jamie stared back just as stubbornly, but Ian's gaze never wavered. At last Jamie sighed and shook his head. "Well, I'm not altogether sure you're right, but even if you are, I can't make any declarations just now, with this circus going on. I'll make it right as soon as we clear out this lot pouring in today."

Ian gazed at him measuringly, recognizing that this postponing of action was uncharacteristic of Jamie.

Jamie looked away. How could he tell Ian that he was afraid? That Sarah was slipping away from him and he didn't know what to do? That his heart froze when he thought about asking her to marry him, for fear she'd say no?

He couldn't ask her until he felt she was ready. If he pushed her too hard, she'd run so far he'd never find her. He felt that kind of withdrawal in her. From the first it had been that way. Push her and she resists. Wait, and she came to him. And right now, after that scene in the woods, she was in full retreat. If he went to her now, he would be cutting his own throat.

It was maddening. He felt he was no closer to understanding the riddle of her than he had been on that first night. What was she afraid of? What did she hide? What kept her just out of his reach? What made her give and give, and then back away?

Her parents' death had made her a loner, that much he understood. There'd never been anyone there for her after the age of nine. That could make a person pathologically independent.

But had it made it impossible for her ever to trust anyone? Ever to settle down? Ever to give any measure of control over her life to another person? If she couldn't live his life, why couldn't she talk to him about it? Why just run away?

On some level he knew she cared about him. But he didn't know what kept them apart. How could he combat something he didn't understand?

Ian was still looking at him. Jamie gazed back at his friend helplessly. There was nothing he could say. He just shrugged. "I'll think about it."

Ian nodded. When Jamie made no further move, he left the room, giving Jamie a harder than necessary brotherly punch on the shoulder in passing.

Thirteen

Spirits ran high that evening. They were reflected in every face Sarah saw, in the laughter, the shouts. Already bottles and flasks were being circulated. After the concert it would be a roistering old party at the inn.

On her way up the stairs to wash and change her rumpled work clothes, Sarah was grabbed from behind and whirled around.

"Sarah!" Jamie said before she could even gasp her surprise. His face was alight with excitement and tension. "You won't forget, will you? Wear the dress." His eyes bored into hers, curiously intent.

She stared down at him, thinking she would jump into the river if he looked at her with the same fierce intensity when he asked.

She shook her head. "I won't forget."

She felt the tension drain out of him. His face softened into a smile that held so much love, she blinked. He nodded, a gesture full of some kind of significance for him. Then with a quick kiss on her forehead, he was off, shouting something to Ian about acoustics on the stage.

Sarah's spirits took an unexpected upswing. She ran upstairs hardly touching the floor.

The dress was at the back of her closet, and she drew it out gently, remembering the look on Jamie's face when he'd bought it for her. That was real. The emotion in that look just couldn't have died completely in so short a time.

She'd wear this dress tonight and she'd stay near him, no matter how many other people tried to come between them. And maybe—just maybe—he'd remember how he'd felt when he'd bought it for her.

When she was ready to go downstairs, Sarah turned slowly in front of the mirror. She looked as perfect as she was capable of looking, and she knew it. Her eyes shone, and a delicate color brushed her cheeks. She wore her hair up, in a style that suited the dress. Escaping curls framed her face becomingly.

Patsy was waiting for her downstairs. "We couldn't have planned it better," she said. "We're perfect foils for each other."

Patsy, too, had her hair swept high, and she was wearing a long, tight black velvet dress that suited her marvelously. "The men had to go on," she said, "but Mary's saving seats for us."

The river was splashing peacefully below the footbridge that led to the amphitheater, and the air was a balmy caress. All around them were voices filled with pleasant anticipation. People were streaming toward the amphitheater from paths in all directions.

Mary waved Sarah and Patsy down to the front row, where she was holding their seats. The place was close to full already. People had come from all over the country, and a number of other countries

162 • SUSAN RICHARDSON

as well, for this festival and this concert in particular. This was a showcase for musicians who were stars in their own part of the entertainment world.

The banks of lights on the slopes of the amphitheater dimmed at last. Applause broke out as Jamie stepped through the curtain into the spotlight.

Sarah and Patsy exchanged amused glances as a teenaged girl behind them said in awed tones, "Look, there's Jamie McLeod! Isn't he gorgeous?"

He was indeed gorgeous, Sarah thought, staring up at him. He was wearing corduroy pants and a blue shirt, as he frequently did, his tie looking—as usual—as if he'd thrown it on as an afterthought. But he commanded everyone's attention. It was his size and lazy grace and something wonderfully alive about him, she decided. He was a little larger than life.

"Good evening." His amplified voice filled the amphitheater with a rich excitement. "I'd like to welcome you all to the first annual Cumberland Mountains Celtic Music Festival."

Whistles, cheers, and applause greeted this announcement.

That was the beginning of three hours of nonstop exhilaration. Jamie, Ian, Guthrie, and Donald opened the program with a set of fast reels that had everyone whooping and clapping in time. In contrast, Peggy's ballads and Gaelic love songs cut straight to the heart. Liam played uillean pipes alone and with his lively group, County Clare.

It was breathtaking, Sarah thought. They'd levitate if they got much higher, and they'd take the audience with them. She hadn't known a crowd's energy could be raised to this level. No wonder Jamie

FIDDLIN' FOOL · 163

said he was addicted to being a musician. What else could compare with it?

But even while she was tapping her foot and swaying, completely caught up in the music, she was waiting. Waiting for Jamie to come onstage again. And waiting for the concert to end so they could be together, so they could talk.

Toward the end of the concert, Jamie came out for a solo number, and Sarah sat forward in her seat.

"This tune," he said into the microphone, "is a recent composition but very much in the Celtic tradition. It's an instrumental number called 'Sarah's.' "

That was all he said, but as he said it he looked directly into Sarah's eyes with an intent appeal.

Sarah felt there was an invisible wire linking them, with electricity zinging back and forth along it. He was twenty feet away from her, but it seemed as if they were touching. Her blood quickened, and her breathing become shallow. He might not want her in his life permanently, but the chemistry between them was incredibly powerful.

Then he began to play.

It was an exultation. That was the only word for it. Jamie's fiddle rang with a wild, triumphant pride that no one could mistake for anything but joy. It was tender, passionate, ecstatic. It was a primitive celebration, and Sarah felt it in every cell of her body.

He loves me! she thought. *I really believe he loves me! If I know anything about music, he's trying to tell me he loves me.*

Hope swept through her like a fever, leaving her shaking and burning at the same time. She wanted so much to believe it; she was so afraid to believe it.

164 • SUSAN RICHARDSON

Beside her, Patsy whispered, "Now do you want to tell me he doesn't care?"

A little hiccoughing laugh broke from Sarah, but she couldn't look away from Jamie.

She was still staring at the space where he'd been, eyes glistening with tears, when all the festival musicians filed onto the stage for the culminating set of the concert—a musicians' session.

They tuned up, then silence fell as Jamie took the microphone.

"Thank you. Thank you all," he said, quieting the hubbub. "To wind up, we'd like to show you a jam session, Celtic-style. Certain melodies and rhythms are common to all Celtic music. We've chosen a number of these for this last group of tunes to show you how remarkably well the different styles of Celtic music blend together."

He waited for the enthusiastic applause to die down. "We hope you've enjoyed the concert and that you'll join us for some of the small-group sessions and workshops scheduled throughout the next few days, as well as for the final concert on Friday. You'll find printed schedules of all festival events in your programs. Thank you again, and good night to you all."

It was routine stuff, but in her exalted state of mind every word was music to Sarah.

The volume of the musicians' session must have been tremendous, but one could hardly hear the music over the clapping of the audience. People were hooting, stamping their feet, and dancing in the aisles, and no one seemed to mind.

When Patsy and Mary grabbed Sarah's hands and swung her with them into the space between the front row and the stage, it seemed the only natural

FIDDLIN' FOOL · 165

outlet for the happiness that was pouring through her. She threw back her head and laughed, a pure, melodic sound.

They were still dancing and she was still laughing when the concert ended and Jamie found her. Somehow his arms replaced Patsy's and Mary's hands, and he was swinging her around in a circle with her feet off the ground. She felt she'd never have to come down. He was laughing too. The breach between them might never have happened.

"Come on," he said. "We've got to go backstage. There's a pre-party party." He towed her through the dispersing crowd into a thicker one backstage. It was a happy throng, everyone still high with the adrenaline of an exceptional performance. People milled around, calling out congratulations and jokes, riding the excitement. Champagne was circulating.

Jamie's arm was around Sarah. She felt a wonderful warmth.

One of the musicians edged by, arms held high to protect two champagne glasses from the crowd. Jamie, using the advantage of his height, reached over and appropriated the glasses from his startled friend.

"For us, Dougal?" he said. "How kind. Thank you." He handed a glass to Sarah with a flourish, ignoring Dougal's open mouth.

Sarah smiled admiringly at Jamie. "Same old manipulative wretch," she complimented him wryly.

In reply he leaned down to claim her lips in a quick, possessive kiss.

She was fascinated by his determined expression, the challenge in his eyes. Jamie, Jamie, she thought. There had never been anyone like Jamie.

Jamie was thinking that he'd not be answerable

166 • SUSAN RICHARDSON

for the consequences if he couldn't get Sarah off to himself soon. His entire body thrummed with frustration. They needed to talk, yes. But his need to touch her was consuming him.

"Jamie! Over here!" It was Ian, shouting and waving above the crowd. Faces turned their way, and others joined in the calling. "Yes, over here. Sarah, come on! They want photographs!"

Jamie scowled his frustration, but there was no getting out of it. "Come on. We'll have to get this over with." He kept a grip on Sarah's wrist as they made their way over to face the press.

This was a group that was used to publicity, so they all posed and shifted with tolerant good humor as they fielded reporters' questions. Jamie received most of the attention, as he was the master of ceremonies. Besides, his book was being made into a major motion picture next month. He was news.

Sarah blinked at the flash bulbs and ping-ponged her head back and forth, trying to follow the disjointed jabbing questions. This was a part of Jamie's life she'd never encountered.

He was handling it well, answering some questions with obliging good humor, blandly ignoring others—the personal ones.

"Who's the pretty lady, McLeod?" was one of the questions that got no answer.

Another reporter, who'd done his homework better, called out, "Miss Hughes! Will we be seeing you on Eilean Mhaol next month?" Sarah might have ignored the question except that Mary next to her, seconded it. "Yes, Sarah, you will be there, won't you?"

Sarah looked up at Jamie, at first confidently expecting his confirmation, or at least an invitation.

He was looking down at her with a strange, rigid expression on his face, a muscle twitching in his cheek. He said nothing. He didn't realize himself that he wasn't breathing.

The reporters, sensing a story, held their questions, but the photographers continued to shoot sporadically. For Sarah, though, they might not have existed. Jamie hadn't answered. Beyond that, what else mattered?

I don't believe this, she thought. *It can't be true.* But as she continued to stare at him and no response came, her smile faltered and faded. She felt as if she were both freezing and burning at the same time.

He didn't want her for the long haul, she thought dully. He wanted her in his bed, but he didn't want to take her home with him.

She was stunned. She couldn't quite take it in. The shock was too great, coming so quickly after her happiness and confidence of a few minutes ago.

Everyone in the group was watching her, and the rowdiness elsewhere cocooned them in a small, quiet place.

Her voice was cool and steady, but to her it sounded very far away. "No, I'll be going home tomorrow."

She hadn't taken her gaze off Jamie. At her words, his breath was expelled as if forced out by a blow. The frozen expression on his face melted into a blazing rage.

In a low, furious voice, he said to her, "I don't know why you bothered to come."

He didn't see her flinch. He looked at the group at large and announced savagely, "Sarah's grown used to temporary arrangements. She actually prefers

168 · SUSAN RICHARDSON

them. I've been a sort of foster boyfriend. But it's not like home, so it's time to move on."

Shock jolted through Sarah's body like an electric current, stopping her breath. As the color drained from her face, her arm jerked involuntarily, spilling champagne down the front of her dress. Aside from that one movement, she was paralyzed. They all were staring in horrified disbelief at Jamie, who was roughly pushing his way out of the group. Cameras flashed. This was a scoop for the tabloids, but there wasn't a reporter brave enough to follow him.

Ian was glaring furiously after Jamie. Patsy looked at Sarah in agonized sympathy. The others were variously embarrassed, aghast, and astonished. Someone uttered a little cry of protest.

Sarah didn't know how she started moving. She couldn't have managed a word, and she was just grateful no one tried to stop her. There were a number of inarticulate murmurs, but she made her escape before anyone recovered enough to act.

Until she reached the woods, she saw everything through a white haze. If someone had tried to stop her, she would have sunk to the ground in a faint, so close was she to unconsciousness. As it was, she was operating on sheer strength of will and her initial momentum.

She ran through the night, past surprised faces and blurring branches. She didn't notice the dogwoods that ripped her dress and scratched her hands. She was fleeing from a lifetime of rejection and helplessness. She had to get away. No one could live with this kind of pain.

A rising wind drove clouds in bursts across the nearly full moon, creating alternating periods of light and darkness. The first drops of rain mingled with

FIDDLIN' FOOL · 169

her tears and splattered on the ground as she gained the cover of the inn.

Back at the stage, Ian hunched his shoulders and bulled his way after Jamie. He caught up with him in the trees behind the stage, grabbed him by the shoulder, and spun him around. "I ought to flatten your nose for you," he said, ignoring the fact that Jamie had five inches and thirty pounds on him.

But then he saw Jamie's face and caught his breath. No blow of his could match the agony Jamie was already feeling. His hand clenched on Jamie's shoulder as rage turned to furious sympathy.

"Ah, you fool! You great, stupid looby. Why don't you just cut yer throat while yer at it? You couldn't do yerself much more harm. And what are you going to do now?"

Fourteen

In her room Sarah was throwing things at random into her suitcase. She could hardly see through the blur of tears, and great sobs forced their way out of her. The frozen numbness had worn off, and now she was feeling.

She whirled when she heard a key in the lock, clutching a shirt to her chest. It was Jamie, swaying a little, with Venetta's master key ring in his hand. His face was ice-white and set.

For a moment he simply stared, registering the tears pouring down her face and the gulps of emotion she couldn't restrain. "Sarah?" he said in wondering concern.

Everything was flooding through Sarah. She couldn't have held back if she'd wanted to, and only a crisis could have made her this forthcoming.

"I'm sorry, I'm sorry," she wailed. "I shouldn't care that it's over. I should have taken it for what it was. I should just have had a wonderful time." Words were being jerked out of her in little gulps and bursts.

170

FIDDLIN' FOOL • 171

"But I couldn't help worrying about the ending. And now it's ending. And I was right to worry. I don't think I can bear it. I'm sorry. I shouldn't have come. I knew I couldn't handle it. It would have been easier to say good-bye in California. And now I've embarrassed you. I'm sorry. I'm sorry."

He had her in his arms, cradling her against his chest. "Shhhh, shhhh, shhhh. You're babbling. Shhhh." His voice was deep and gentle. "Hush, now. You're making no sense." Laughter threaded his words. "If you say *sorry* once more, I'll be forced to do you an injury. I've just been a total brute, and you're saying sorry?"

But she couldn't stop crying. Little cries of pain kept breaking from her. She wasn't even hearing him.

He lifted her up and lay on the bed with her, cradling her, stroking, soothing. "Shhh, shhh," he said over and over. "I love you, I love you, *mo cridhe, mo cridhe.*"

At length her sobs subsided and his words penetrated. "What did you say?" she whispered weakly.

"I said I love you. I said you're my heart and my life."

"Why are you saying that?" It was a cry of anguish.

"Because it's true."

She shook her head. "You don't want me." Her voice held total certainty.

"I don't?" he asked, tender and amused.

"Not for long. You don't want me on Eilean Mhaol."

He looked at her in amazement. "You're daft. You knew I did."

She stared at him through swollen eyes, a little spark of hope flickering inside her. "You never invited me."

"Of course I did!"

172 • SUSAN RICHARDSON

She shook her head.

His astonishment slowly turned to uncertainty. "But you knew." It was more a question than a statement.

Again she shook her head.

He looked even more uncertain. "Perhaps I didn't say it. But it never occurred to me I'd need to. I've been trying to say it every way I know how. I'm not so good with words. But could you not feel from my music for you how much I love you?"

She nodded, but pain was still in her eyes. "Yes, I could tell you love me." He waited for her to go on. She bit her lip. "Love and commitment are the same thing for me," she explained slowly. "But I've learned that commitment's much rarer for most people than love is. I thought you were like that."

"Ah, Sarah," he murmured in anguish. "I was just waiting for you to make up your mind if you could stand my scrambling lifestyle. I thought you knew I wanted you for always."

She should have found this reassuring, but anguish twisted inside her. "No one has ever wanted me for always," she said when she could speak. "I don't really belong anywhere. You weren't sure I'd fit in her or on Eilean Mhaol. And I don't."

He let her cry softly while he stared at her, thinking. He knew he was hearing old refrains.

"Sarah," he said finally. "It's in my mind that I'm fighting other people's battles. Who didn't want you? Where didn't you think you fit in?"

Her face twisted as out of long habit she resisted talking about it. But her defenses were well down. It burst out of her. "No one wanted me!" she said passionately. "I lived with eight different families,

FIDDLIN' FOOL • 173

not counting the ones that kept me less than a week, and not one of them wanted me."

Jamie was incredulous. Eight? his mind echoed in outrage. Sarah didn't notice his shock. She was reliving it all.

"I tried so hard to fit in! I was pleasant and cooperative. I was undemanding. But it was never enough. There must have been something lacking in me." Her voice reflected the bewilderment she must have felt as a child.

He gave her a sharp little shake. "Don't ever say that!" he commanded fiercely. "There's nothing lacking in you. Nothing! The lack was in the homes—a lack of generosity. Or maybe they knew you were far too good for them!"

Sarah blinked. She'd never had this kind of absolute championing. It was such a different perspective from the one she'd carried with her most of her life that she stopped to consider it, surprised.

Jamie pressed his advantage. "You're rather unique, you know. You wouldn't fit in just anywhere. It would take a very special place to match you, and very special people. Rather like me," he added whimsically. He invited her to smile with him.

She didn't smile, but the color of her eyes changed as he watched, from almost black to a silvery gray. The clouds were lifting. "Can you see that that might be true?" he asked gently.

Sarah looked wonderingly at this man who could change her world around with a few words. Warmth was beginning to glow somewhere deep inside her. "I can see that there might be another way of looking at it," she conceded.

He grinned and relaxed slightly. "It's that that's

174 • SUSAN RICHARDSON

been going on this entire week, isn't it?" he asked. "My guess is that leaving your home and friends triggered all these childhood insecurities."

She thought about that. "You may be right. On some level I think I knew I was being absurd, but that made it worse. I wanted so much to make you happy, and I kept acting like a jealous, insecure teenager."

"I don't know about that," he said. "I thought you were just indifferent to me."

She stared at him. "I suppose that was because I was trying so hard not to let you see how much I needed you."

He framed her face with his large hands and looked at her very seriously. "Sarah, my darling. You have to believe that I know how strong you are. No one could have lived through your childhood and come out so loving and giving if she wasn't strong. You must never be afraid of needing me. Will you promise me that? Lord knows I need you. I'm not proud. I'll beg you. Please, Sarah. Don't leave me. If you have to have a permanent home, we'll find you one. Nothing in the world is as important to me as you. When I thought you were pulling out on me, back there at the amphitheater, I wanted to destroy the whole world."

She gazed at him in wonder. Excitement was beginning to fizz and bubble in her veins. He wanted her. He'd always wanted her. All his reservations had been on her account. And here he was, this strong Jamie of hers, thinking she had to be eased and wooed into his lifestyle, all because she was too insecure—too proud—to show him her love.

"Jamie," she breathed, raising her hands to cra-

FIDDLIN' FOOL • 175

dle his face in turn. "You're my home. Don't you know that? That's what I was so afraid of. I spent so much time and effort carving out a niche for myself, and you came along and made it all mean nothing. You're the home I've always wanted. I don't care about anything else."

His eyes searched her face anxiously. "Are you sure, Sarah? I can't promise you luxury or even real financial security." The humility in his voice made her heart ache.

"That's okay. I wasn't for sale anyway," she said to take him out of this painful seriousness. He rewarded her with a smile. "Besides," she continued, "a composer, musician, author, master of ceremonies, and festival organizer who's becoming known through television and films wouldn't sound like a bad prospect to the most dedicated gold digger."

He recognized her attempts to build him up. "That's right," he agreed. "Besides, I forgot you're a celebrated authoress. We'll use your royalties to make life bearable."

She tilted her head to look measuringly at him. She needed to scotch this idea he had that she would be making a great sacrifice to marry him, once and for always. "Yes, that's true," she said agreeably. "If we discover that a life full of music, laughter, excitement, travel, friendship, and love are inadequate, we'll use the royalties to buy all the designer labels, decorator items, and VCR high-resolution, fast-track, multilevel gadgets without which no self-respecting American can be happy."

He smiled wryly. "Aye, go ahead, mock me," he said in a martyred tone. More seriously, he added, "But you forget I've heard a number of women expounding on the subject of being a musician's wife.

176 • SUSAN RICHARDSON

It doesn't come out a eulogy. You yourself noticed how much time and attention you get when I'm working. I'm a demanding bastard then."

"If all these women hate the life so much," she said quietly, "why do they live it?"

He looked at her strangely. "Ah, a trap." She waited. Slowly, he said, "Because they love their men and have no choice, really."

Sarah's smile was her comment.

"Do you love me that much, Sarah?" he asked with humility and wonder.

Her smile grew wider. "You are a fool," she said tenderly, pressing her forehead against his and looking into his eyes. "A fiddin' fool."

Their lips met in a gentle, passionless gesture of perfect understanding. It was an entire conversation in itself.

At length Jamie pulled back to smile at her. "Well, while we're on the subject of fools," he said, "I know one can't have everything—and you are beautiful, after all—but where did you get this foolish, idiotic notion that I cared two damns whether or not you 'fit in' anywhere?"

She tilted her head questioningly. Did he really not remember? "From that first night you told me you were falling in love with me. And you were so disgusted, because the road was hard and Eilean Mhaol was no place for someone who wasn't raised there." She spoke flippantly, but her voice faintly mirrored the hurt she had felt then.

"Ah," he said, understanding finally. "I was sure, wasn't I?" He stared past her for a moment, then his mouth quirked. "Well, even I, you know, am fallible."

"It's a good thing you're smiling."

He ignored that. "We've been over this, haven't we?" he asked, looking at her seriously. "You understand that I didn't doubt you could fit into my life, I just doubted if you'd want to."

She nodded, but she had one lingering doubt. "What about the islanders not taking to outsiders?" She turned onto one side and propped her head on her hand.

"It's only people who don't share island values that never settle in there," he explained. "Giving people and tasks due consideration, for instance, is more important there than being punctual or saving time. And island courtesy means never pushing, always respecting other peoples' boundaries." He turned his head to look fondly at her. "You were born with Hebridean values."

She warmed to his smile, but she was still thinking. "What about your family?" she asked. "How are they likely to feel about your marrying an American?"

"Sarah, don't you understand yet? For one thing, my family means nothing to me next to you. For another, these"—he waved to indicate the musicians all around them—"are my family. For two thirds of the year. And for the rest, they're no different from those at home. Did you not know that Donald is my cousin? And Ian is as close to me as a brother."

She smiled. She felt warm and happy inside, like a cat in an angora blanket. It was hard to imagine that she could feel any more secure and relaxed than she did right now. But for the sake of discussion, she said, "What about your grandmother?"

"I'll tell you a secret about my granny. She's my greatest conquest. The first of a long line of women who'd leap into the sea for a smile from me."

Sarah fell back onto the mattress, groaning. "Oh, the ego! The overwhelming ego!"

"Yes," he continued blandly. "You mustn't think you're unique in your total devotion to pleasing me—

178 • SUSAN RICHARDSON

Oof!" he grunted as Sarah's slim body hurled itself on top of him.

He spanned her waist with his hands and continued. "There, see, you knew just what would please me, what did I tell you?" He grinned up at her. "I didn't even have to ask."

Sarah's smile softened as she absorbed the warmth in his eyes. "You'll never have to ask," she promised him.

"That's good," he said. His voice had changed. It wasn't relaxed any longer, but low and tense. "Because if I had to ask tonight, it would come out begging. Do you have any idea how I'm longing to touch you?"

"I think I have some idea," she teased.

"Do you have any more questions for me?"

"No more questions," she whispered. The time for kidding had passed.

One big hand cradled the back of her neck to pull her head down. It held her just inches from his face as their breath mingled, warm and moist, and their gazes roamed and searched. Sarah could feel longing building to fever pitch between them.

When the pressure on her neck eased, she lowered her head the rest of the way to his, sighing her satisfaction. With the contact of their lips, Jamie's body gave a galvanic leap. Sarah felt the same stab of desire sear through her stomach.

A sound of shock escaped from her throat, then changed to a little growl as Jamie increased the pressure on her head to deepen the kiss. A trembling started inside her as she slid her lips back and forth across his.

He let her go, and his head fell back onto the mattress as he gasped for air and grasped for control. "Sarah, Sarah," he said in that wondering way he had.

FIDDLIN' FOOL · *179*

"Yes," she whispered, her entire body quivering with feeling.

He pulled her down onto him so he could reach behind her for her dress buttons. She lay still but smiled when she felt one fly off. A frustrated laugh gusted out of his chest.

"Whose idea was it to buy a dress with a thousand tiny buttons, anyway?"

"Yours," she breathed.

"Turn around," he commanded, raising her to a sitting position.

She lowered her head while his fingers busied themselves at her back. "My beautiful dress," she said mournfully, noting the rips and stains down the front of it. "It's ruined."

He kissed the nape of her neck and the part of her back exposed by his efficient fingering. "It's served its purpose, hasn't it? You know, I meant it for a wedding dress. Tonight's our real wedding, isn't it? Whatever follows, this is our nuptial night." The timbre of his voice against her skin left no doubt about his sincerity. Her eyes closed with her happiness.

The bedraggled lace slid away from her body, and Jamie quickly dealt with undergarments and hairpins, sliding his fingers through her hair to free it. He turned her to face him. She raised her head, lips parted, and he sighed heavily as his gaze caressed her.

Outside, the storm was coming closer. Silvery light through the window created almost a strobe effect on Sarah's body as clouds sped across the moon. A flash of lightning outlined her flesh in brilliant detail, and Jamie caught his breath.

"It's been a fantasy of mine to love you during a storm," he said huskily. At the longing in his voice, her body vibrated, swept into the fantasy with him.

180 · SUSAN RICHARDSON

A breeze from the partially open window lifted her hair on cue and swirled strands across her face. She laughed, intoxicated with a sense of power. A faint boom of thunder reached them, like a counterpoint to her laughter.

His hands rose to his own buttons, but she gently shoved them aside. "I want to do that," she said in a throaty voice. He answered with a strangled moan.

She made it a slow disrobing, taking time to appreciate the play of moonlight and shadow over Jamie's fair skin, the silver gleam of moon-haloed hair and hair-dusted limbs. "You're magnificent," she murmured, stroking his broad shoulders and hard chest.

Her fingertips explored the definitions of Jamie's muscles, the creases in his cheeks. His mouth fascinated her. It was long and firm. While his eyes communicated a steady warmth, the mouth put in the shadings: warm liking, warm amusement, warm irony, warm scorn, warm devilment. At the moment it was communicating warm wonder.

"Jamie," she whispered, rubbing her cheek against his chest. She felt the tension building, the trembling starting in his limbs, and marveled that he could be so vulnerable.

Jamie had had enough of being passive. He reached for her, controlling himself with difficulty, and carefully reacquainted himself with the shapes of her breasts, shoulders, and arms. He watched her eyes grow slumberous and loved the piquant heart shape of her face.

When she lay back on the bed, inviting him to follow her, he stood and gathered all their clothes into a bundle. He tossed them to a chair, explaining, "I don't want anything in my field of vision but you."

FIDDLIN' FOOL · 181

She smiled, and he stood where he was for a moment, feeling a constriction in his chest at the picture she made. She lay at peace on her side, all doubts and insecurities at rest. Her eyes were wide and mysterious, her body flowing, uninterrupted curves and unconscious allure. *Is she finally mine?* he asked himself in wonder, hardly daring to believe it. *Is she through running?*

She held out her hand, and he went to her and took her in his arms. He began to kiss her, his hands soothing and smoothing over her satiny back and buttocks.

Love flowed out of her in a stream. She felt like hot metal, expanding and melting. She abandoned her mind to the pleasures her body was communicating to it.

Their soft moans and sighs as they caressed and pressed their bodies together provided a counterpoint to the now steady drone of rain on the roof just above them.

Ah, Jamie, Sarah thought, sighing. Your hands. Your magical hands.

She became aware that his hands were trembling, and in a flash she realized something she'd never noticed before. The control. Jamie was exercising—had always exercised—careful control with her, putting his needs on hold as he wooed and seduced her from her fears!

Ah, Jamie! Remorse and gratitude poured through her. Didn't he know it was different now? She would have to show him.

She tangled her slim fingers in his silvery thatch, then tightened them to catch his attention. Shifting to hover over him, she let her eyes burn into his widening blue gaze until he tensed, sensing the

182 · SUSAN RICHARDSON

change in her. Then she lowered her mouth, hot and open and wanton.

Jamie growled deep in his throat as the force of her arousal washed over him. His arms clutched her back, and she was rolling under, then over, then under him again, tumbled in the full surge of his male needs.

She laughed low in her throat, reveling in it. She was discovering that opening to Jamie was as natural and simple as breathing. She had nothing she wouldn't give him, share with him.

"Sarah!" he cried joyfully. Here it was, then, he realized, the warmth, the passion he'd sensed in her from the first, swirling unfettered around him. It had been there before, but grudgingly, in spite of the brakes she applied to it. Now it was a flowering, onrushing river of female power, and everything primevally male in him rushed up to meet it.

He followed his own urges without censorship for the first time, knowing that the days were past when he had to pursue and gentle her, knowing that she could match him power for power, raw urgency for raw urgency. She had led him to this place.

Sarah's mind was spinning in a turbulence she couldn't have forseen. It was helplessness and triumph all at once. It was trust and total surrender. It was a freedom beyond imagining to loose the torrents of love she'd kept banked all her life. This trembling and shuddering was a weakness that was no weakness, a need that was a satisfaction of a long-stifled imperative—to love and be loved without barriers or restraints.

As Jamie reared over her, she welcomed him home. They were both home, all wandering ended. Here was where they belonged. She rode the rapids fearlessly, giving herself to each dip and crest as they plunged to shattering completion.

Sarah's excitement was so intense that she thought later she must have blacked out for a few seconds, because when consciousness returned she was atop Jamie, her hands cupping his face.

He was looking up at her with love and wonder in his eyes. His face—all his body—was wet with perspiration.

Her hair hung down on either side of them in feathery curtains, making a shadowy, private bower for their faces. It was incredibly intimate as they remained suspended in the aftermath of overwhelming pleasure.

"Welcome home," he said softly.

She smiled. "Are you going to read my mind all the time from now on?"

He smiled too. "It might have saved a bit of trouble if I'd started earlier. I probably could have, too, if I hadn't been so unsure of myself."

"You? Unsure of yourself?" she murmured in disbelief.

"Aye, where you're concerned. It's always mattered too much. You warp my perspective." He didn't sound as if he minded. It was desultory conversation, expressing total contentment and not much else.

She lay her head on his chest, and he rolled so they were side by side.

For a few minutes they gazed at each other as they listened to the rain and the wind. They had sounded like teardrops and moaning to Sarah earlier. Now they represented cleansing and singing. The storm outside was no more than contrast for the warmth inside.

184 • SUSAN RICHARDSON

But if the rain had been no more to them than a musical accompaniment to their loving, it had had a greater effect on the ancient slate roof. The water had worked its way through assorted passageways in the roof, and soon they could no longer ignore it.

"Damn it all!" Jamie yelped as cold drips assaulted his bare back. He rolled to one side, carrying a chuckling Sarah with him.

"Do you realize," he complained, "that I manage to make love to you with impunity only about one in three times? The rest of the time I pay with a soaking."

Her sympathetic murmur was somewhat diluted by the low gurgle of laughter that accompanied it. "Poor Jamie."

"Oh-ho, so you think it's funny, do you, my little water sprite, my fine mermaid, my aqueous lover." He loomed threateningly over her, pretending fierce resentment.

"I'm perfectly safe," she gloated unwisely. "Look at the size of my umbrella."

His teasing turned to tenderness and fire as he looked down at her radiant face. Lord, he felt he'd sell his soul to keep her looking like that. Abandoning the game, he lowered himself slowly onto her. The leak was a fairly localized one, he thought. They could avoid it.

"Consider this a measure of my devotion," he said in a low, soft voice. "Right now I'm quite sure I'm about to drown. But will it stop me? It will not."

Sarah's only response was a sigh of ecstasy.

Into her ear Jamie murmured, "And I'm definitely going to call my next album *Drowning*."

THE EDITOR'S CORNER

Next month is an important landmark for all of us on the LOVESWEPT team—our fourth birthday! I received an absolutely wonderful letter a few months ago, and I decided to wait until now to share it with you, because its message is a real birthday tribute to LOVESWEPT. The letter came from a woman and her husband who have been married a long time. He is enthusiastic about televised sports; she is a romance reader who counts LOVESWEPT her favorite line. One Sunday afternoon while he was engrossed watching a game, his wife sat nearby reading a LOVESWEPT and chuckling and laughing aloud at various passages. Fortunately, her husband didn't get annoyed, only curious, and later that night he asked if he could borrow the book she had so obviously enjoyed. She loaned it to him. He loved it. He asked to read more of those "terrific stories." Their letter—a joint effort—thanked us not only for entertaining them so much, but also for helping to put a whole lot of new zing and zip into their relationship. I treasure this letter, as I treasure so many you've written to me through the years.

So what do we have for you on our birthday month? An especially merry—perhaps inspiring?—quartet of romances.

First, in talented Joan Elliott Pickart's **WILD POPPIES,** LOVESWEPT #190, you'll encounter a simply delightful couple. Heroine Courtney Marshall, a lovely young widow, decides she must go on a husband hunt to provide her two small children with a sweet, reliable father. Luke Hamilton is a gorgeous hunk of man who doesn't appear to be the least bit steady to Courtney so she immediately rules him out and tells him the reason! Luke is floored by Courtney's "quest" and more than a little worried about the fate of such a beautiful and innocent soul out there in the woods with all those big, bad wolves. (And Luke should

(continued)

know—he has howled with the best of them!) Protecting and pleasing Courtney are priorities for Luke that soon turn to fiery passion in this love story whose charms will linger with you for many a day.

Who would guess that behind the pretty face, just under the lovely blond hair of Iris Johansen lurks a whole universe of people, places, adventures, and love with all its joys and a few of its sorrows? A stranger wouldn't guess but all of us know, right? And next month Iris will tour you through places you've visited with her before and she'll reacquaint you with a few old friends while she delights you anew with a marvelous romance, **ACROSS THE RIVER OF YESTERDAY,** LOVESWEPT #191. Part cowboy, part cavalier, and all man, Gideon Brandt knew his footloose days were numbered the very second he saw violet-eyed Serena Spaulding. But Serena was bound to others by secrets and responsibilities that forced her to hide from Gideon for years. He'd searched the wide world for her . . . and when he recaptured her at last it was hardly the ideal place or time for a love to flourish. Yet, even as their very lives were threatened, their desire for each other blazed to white heat . . . a sensational love story!

Witty, whimsical, passionate are the words that readily describe **THE JOY BUS,** LOVESWEPT #192, by the very creative Peggy Webb. Ms. Jessie Wentworth, mistress of all she surveys and a workaholic of the first order, is alternately baffled and beguiled by devastatingly handsome Blake Montgomery. Blake is a professor using his sabbatical for meandering through the countryside and putting on the magic shows he finds such fun to do, all out of his pink touring bus! Wonderfully down to earth—and earthy!—Blake makes Jessie see stars—and even wish on them. But how could she be sure that their love for one another wasn't just another illusion? JOY BUS is—truly—a joy!

(continued)

The book Kay Harper has created for you for next month is so fast-paced, so full of surprises, so breathtaking in the passionate intensity of its romance, that the best place for you to read it would be in a plane because you'd have a seat belt and a ready supply of pure oxygen! Find the next best spot to settle in and fly away even without a plane with **RAVEN ON THE WING,** LOVESWEPT #193. The hero is a man you know very well from **IN SERENA'S WEB,** LOVESWEPT #189 this month. Joshua Long avoids brunettes as if they carried the plague, as you'll recall. He will only date blondes and Serena has clued us into the reason: Josh knows the woman of his dreams will be a brunette . . . and she'll put an end to his playboy days. His intuition was right. He meets his loving fate in the sexy shape of Raven Anderson, a woman as beautiful as she is enigmatic. When the maddeningly mysterious Raven disappears, Josh has to use all the formidable tools he can bring to hand . . . and in the process almost destroys the woman he only wants to cherish. This is a riveting love story!

I hope that in the year to come not one of our LOVESWEPTS will disappoint you.

Warm regards,

Carolyn Nichols

Carolyn Nichols
  Editor
LOVESWEPT
Bantam Books, Inc.
666 Fifth Avenue
New York, NY 10103

NEW!
Handsome Book Covers Specially Designed To Fit Loveswept Books

Our new French Calf Vinyl book covers come in a set of three great colors—royal blue, scarlet red and kachina green.

Each 7" × 9½" book cover has two deep vertical pockets, a handy sewn-in bookmark, and is soil and scratch resistant.

To order your set, use the form below.

ORDER FORM
STX
YES! Please send me

_____ set(s) of three book covers at $5.95 per set. Enclosed is my check/money order for the full amount. (Price includes postage and handling; NY and IL residents, please add appropriate sales tax.) 09605

Ship To:

_____
Name   (Please Print)

_____
Address

_____
City   State   Zip

Send Order To: Bantam Books, Merchandise Division
P.O. Box 956
Hicksville, NY 11802

Prices in U.S. dollars   Satisfaction Guaranteed
                                          STX—3 87